THE DAY IT ALL CHANGED

THE DAY IT ALL CHANGED

VIKRAM SINGH

NU VOICE
PRESS

First published by NU VOICE PRESS 2025
An imprint of Hubhawks Pvt. Ltd
www.nuvoicepress.com

This is a work of fiction and all characters and incidents described in this book are the product of the author's imagination. Any resemblance to actual persons, living or dead, is entirely coincidental.

ISBN: 978-81-982661-3-2

Typeset by Saanvi Graphics, Noida
Printed at Thomson Press India Private Limited
Published by Nu Voice Press

Prologue

The final hooter sounded as I embarked on my maiden train journey in India. Gazing out of the glass window, the ever-chaotic Delhi station platform seemed so peaceful. Clean and comfortable, the Rajdhani Express had been a good choice so far!

"Hi, can I keep my bag underneath your seat?" asked the gentleman who managed to board the train just in time.

"Why not? There's enough space in the cabin. The other two passengers may have changed their minds," I replied reluctantly.

"Or perhaps missed the train," said my co-passenger with a smile. "Thank God, my cabby knew the shortest route. You can never trust Delhi traffic. Sorry! Forgot to introduce myself."

"My name is Yogesh! I teach meditation at Rishikesh, so people call me Yogi."

"Hello! I am John. I am a publisher and a fiction writer." This brief introduction was followed by a handshake.

I felt welcomed.

"Is this your first trip to India? What brings you here?"

I was being bombarded with questions. We writers like to talk only when the subject is of interest to us. Nevertheless, I decided to respond.

"First trip, actually. Came here to experience the cradle of spirituality and this is the last leg of my journey," I replied, reflecting his smile.

"Interesting. That's the writer in you speaking. Your accent tells me that you are American. Looks like there will be a lot to talk about," said Yogi smugly.

"You do have good ears, sir. Normally, people recognize Americans by their plus-size clothes, ha ha. Seems like I have met my match," I mumbled.

"That said, I am intrigued by your personality. At first, I thought you were some corporate honcho. It's hard to imagine a clean-shaven spiritual guru dressed in jeans and a polo t-shirt." I was slowly opening up.

"Appearances can often be deceptive, John. And let me tell you, clothes have nothing to do with spirituality. It's about aligning your mind with the soul. Nothing else matters!"

"So true! I think my journey in search of a guru has ended and to tell you the truth, this was my main reason for travelling to India. I knew it the moment I looked into your deep eyes."

"Thank you, John. That's the best compliment I have ever received for my eyes. Ha ha!"

"So, are you going to Dibrugarh on a sightseeing trip?"

"Actually, I am going to Varanasi. Can't go back to New York without experiencing that oasis of spirituality."

"So, we have a common destination too. You are right, John! A trip to India would be incomplete without the experience of mystical Kashi."

"Oh! Someone is knocking at the cabin door. Let me see." Yogi quickly got up to slide the door open.

"It's the cabin attendant. Wants to know our choice of beverage. Tea, for me, would be a great way to start a 13-hour journey. How about you, John? Tea or coffee?"

"I don't mean to be rude, but coffee, to me, is only Starbucks. So, I will go for tea without sugar, and some cookies too."

"What exactly are you seeking here in India? Any luck so far?" asked Yogi.

"You mean subjectively or objectively?" I winked.

"See, that's the problem with you writers! You can never answer in simple words." Yogi laughed.

"Oh yes, that's one of our occupational hazards. Actually, I came here for a break, but soon realized that the best break for a fiction writer would be writing non-fiction."

"So, here I am. Travelling in your beautiful country, looking for a story! Ha ha." I grinned like a Cheshire cat. "So far, I have enjoyed every moment of my stay in India. This place is so mysterious!"

"I couldn't agree more, John. There is so much to experience here that everyone can write at least one book in a lifetime. In fact, I too have a story in mind. Hopefully, I will be able to write it someday!"

"A story? Wow! Fiction or non-fiction? Can you share the excerpt with me?" The mere mention of the word 'story' was enough to ignite my curiosity.

"Why only an excerpt, my friend? I will share the entire story with you! But you will have to wait for the genre, because I don't want to kill the suspense. I am sure you will have a better understanding of life after you finish hearing it."

"Thanks, Yogi! Although I have no reason to doubt it, but if it is interesting enough, I will be happy to ghost write this book for you. I am all ears now!"

Chapter 1

Krish moved to Mumbai to pursue his dream of becoming the youngest tech millionaire. Born into a middle-class family, he was exceedingly good at football. His loving but overbearing parents did not allow him to follow that path. Sports, to them, was a sheer waste of time, and teenage years were best spent with books.

After pursuing his Computer Engineering from IIT Delhi, Krish took up a job as a software engineer in Hyderabad. He moved to three different cities in fifteen years before finally settling down in Mumbai.

He finally resigned from his job, in pursuit of his entrepreneurial ambitions, to set up RoverSoft, his own software company.

His wife, Mira, was the first girl he had ever dated, that too after seeking permission from his parents. Mira was a well-educated lady bestowed with good looks, strong family values and a controlling mother. It was no wonder, that both his kids were extremely disciplined.

His friend, Tony, was one of the biggest influences in his life. A rebel by cause and Protestant by religion, his grandparents had migrated to Mumbai from Kerala.

Wonder what Krish liked about this high-school-dropout-vodka-crazy-womanizer? Such a lost soul he was and pretty confused about his existence too. He had become a wreck after his parents' separation and got addicted to drugs. Poor lad, it took two visits to the rehab centre to get him back on track.

His family owned a grocery store which grossed one of the highest sales in Mumbai. Tony was never a business person and given a chance, would sell the entire store and travel the world.

Not all those who wander are lost, though. Tony had a tinge of spirituality in him that he owed to a Tibetan Buddhist monk, Dorjee, whom he had met through a common friend.

He always wondered how a simple monk from the mountains could attain such a sense of satisfaction, as all he could afford was a couple of yellow robes and three basic meals a day.

Asif was their third partner in crime. His father came from Agra to become a priest in a suburban Mosque. Though he had been brought up in a conservative environment, he was a free soul. The family survived on his father's paltry income. At his father's persuasion, he tried his hand at selling Afghani carpets, but couldn't make it big. He couldn't have, because music was his first love.

His father, an honest man and a devout Muslim, spent most of his life preaching at the local mosque. Asif was completely the opposite; his Western education had given him a very liberal bent of mind.

Chapter 2

It was one of those Friday evenings. Everyone seemed so happy and excited. We all love our weekends!

It was time to drink, eat like a glutton, and the best part, one didn't have to report for work the next day.

Asif was playing basketball with the teenagers who were hustling their way to join the local basketball club and play for the State team someday.

On the basketball court, Asif also behaved like a teenager, playing with them, listening to hip-hop and shaking his body whenever he would dunk.

Krish was going back to his apartment after dropping his wife and kids at the airport. They were going to Krish's home in Varanasi.

His father was desperate to meet his grandchildren, and there was also a family wedding that could not be missed.

Krish could not join his family as he was expecting a delegation from Europe in three weeks and needed to sign a major deal with them.

This could be his biggest contract ever, and all the sweat and toil that he and his partner had put in all these years was finally going to pay off.

If the deal went through, they were going to make a fortune. He had already planned on buying an apartment in downtown Colaba, an expensive sports car, and become a part of the Indian elite.

He parked his car in the garage and went for a stroll in the neighbourhood. On any other day, he would have rushed inside the house and fallen on the couch in his living room. Mira would bring a hot cup of his favourite ginger tea over which they would share their day's happenings.

While out on his stroll he walked by the basketball court and saw Asif playing with the boys.

"Hey dude, what's up?" asked Krish.

"Nothing much. How about you?" replied Asif as he passed the ball to another player.

"Asif, would you like to join me for a drink tonight?"

"Sure, bro. Let me finish this last game and then I am all yours."

"In the meantime, why don't you check with Tony to see if he is available too?"

"Why not, the more the merrier!" replied Krish with a broad smile exhibiting all his teeth.

"Asif and I are planning on going clubbing and it would be wonderful if you could join us too." Krish quickly called Tony so that he didn't make other plans for the evening.

"Sure! Which club? Tell me the plan." Tony was excited as hell.

"Ahem...Trance Fever. Have you been there? Asif told me it's a great place!"

"Wow! That sounds great! Yes, I have been there; just love their live band. Would it be ok if I join you guys at 11.30 p.m.?" asked Tony.

"Sounds good," said Krish and hung up.

Tony's father had asked him not to close the store before 11 p.m. as Friday evenings always guaranteed maximum footfall. The store was opened by his grandfather as a small shop, and his father had turned it into one of the most successful grocery stores in town. He did not expect Tony to grow it further and was more than happy if his son was just able to sustain the business.

That evening was special, because the three friends were meeting after months. Tony's eyes were glued to the clock hanging in front of the payment counter, just above the rack full of gums and jellies.

"Sorry ma'am! Its 11 p.m.; the store is closed."

It's never easy to say no to customers who pop in at the last moment but that night, Tony didn't care. Images of a fun filled evening was all he could think of.

He once again checked the cash, switched off the computer and closed the shop.

The club was full of pretty girls with perfectly toned bodies, dressed to kill. The menfolk too wanted to leave an impression, and were neatly dressed with gelled hair.

At the right-hand corner, near the bar, was a group of geeks sipping their beers and discussing the latest in technology, artificial intelligence, big data, and more.

The early starters had moved from beer to Scotch and were already drooling.

"Guys, sorry I'm late. This place is rocking tonight, I am sure the beautiful women at the bar kept you guys busy," said Tony winking at them. He ordered his favourite Screwdriver with extra ice.

A few drinks down, the music was getting louder. Hard rock was something no one could resist; it was time to hit the dance floor and they all started swaying to the music.

Alcohol and good music are undoubtedly the most intoxicating combination. The DJ was doing a fabulous job, moving from hard rock to trance. It was pure ecstasy!

Out of nowhere came a bulky bouncer and asked Krish to step off dance floor. Apparently one of the girls on the floor had complained to one of the managers that he was swaying all over.

This wasn't his normal behaviour. But who cared tonight? He was drunk and his wife was not at home; tonight he had no inhibitions.

The manager told them to immediately leave the dance floor as it was causing discomfort to the other guests.

This is the last thing you want to happen on a perfectly fun-filled Friday night.

"Can't believe this! We have been thrown out of the pub," Tony said as he stepped out with a heavy heart.

"Man! This is crazy. We had just started enjoying the music. Krish, this is entirely your fault," Asif complained.

"C'mon guys, I didn't do it on purpose. I was a few drinks down and was enjoying the music; just lost my balance, that's all!"

"Yes, but only thrice," chuckled Asif.

"Asif, you are such a moron," said Krish biting his teeth. "This isn't the only club in town. Let's go to another pub, shall we?"

"Yes," both Tony and Asif replied in unison.

"But who is going to drive now? The nearest pub is ten kilometres from here," said Krish, resting his head on his hands.

"Let's not be thrown out of a pub and put behind bars all in the same night."

"Hey! Let's go to the park and discuss this," said Asif pointing towards the community park.

While they lay on the park bench gazing at the stars, an idea struck Tony. "Guys, shall we plan a trip to Goa?" he asked.

"The oasis of pleasure! Believe me, it's going to be the trip of a lifetime. What say?"

"Oh yes! A trip to our own Sin City can only cool us down now. Beautiful glitter, fun loving people, and no narrow-minded women. I am game for it," said Asif. "But this should be longer than our previous weekend outings. Man! Going all the way and coming back in two days isn't that much fun."

"How about you, Krish?" asked Tony.

"Sorry guys. I would love to visit Goa with you guys, but I have a very important business meeting in three weeks and I still have a great deal of preparation to take care of," replied a rather disappointed Krish.

"C'mon bro. Don't ruin it. Just imagine a week full of pure fun."

"Drinks, great food, women, gambling, etc., all in one place. It doesn't get better than this!"

"I have been there before and believe me there is nothing like Goa," said Tony, trying to convince Krish.

"It's just one week and you will still be left with two weeks more to do your office work," Asif cajoled.

"Don't you remember we have always wanted to go there? This is the best time, even your family is not here so there's no one to stop you. This is it! We will not get such an opportunity again!" he continued.

Twenty minutes of hard persuasion and Krish was ready to capitulate. Even before his confirmation the blokes started to jump. Guess that's what happens after years of friendship.

It was already past midnight and the plan was to travel the next day. They decided to go back to their homes and catch some sleep.

Krish agreed to book the air tickets and the hotel before hitting the sack.

It was a bright, sunny day and their flight was in the afternoon. Considering the distance, driving wouldn't have been a good option.

Having gone through the airport check-in formalities and some last-minute shopping, they finally boarded the flight and took their seats.

Due to their last-minute booking, they couldn't get all three seats together. Tony had to sit separately in an aisle seat.

Maybe that was his destiny; his seat was next to an interesting and elegant middle-aged lady called Laila, who was a Tarot reader by profession. She had come to Mumbai to visit her sister.

"So, you are going to Goa for some entertainment, eh?" asked Laila, starting up a conversation.

"Yes ma'am, but how did you know?" a surprised Tony asked.

"Well, that's why most people visit Goa. I, too, went there for fun, twenty years ago, with my boyfriend. Initially, we had planned to stay for a week but after spending a few days there I realized this is the place for me and planned to stay back."

"My boyfriend didn't like the idea and asked me to either go back with him, or to forget him, and guess what, I chose Goa. That's the magic of this place."

"Here I am, taking Tarot card and face reading classes, successfully, in this Sin City for the last two decades." She smiled.

"That's interesting. In fact, we too are going for a week but we definitely plan to return to Mumbai," said Tony.

"Oh! Really? This is an all-boy's trip, isn't it?" winked Laila.

"Yes, but how did you know?"

"Well, you wouldn't be sitting next to me if you had a girlfriend with you. But don't worry, you will find plenty of them over there," said Laila with a laugh and her deep blue eyes sparkled a little more.

"That's smart!" replied Tony with a sheepish smile.

"I don't know much about Tarot reading and stuff. All I can remember is what my grandmother told me when I was a child about this famous prophecy of the French guy Nostradamus, who came into the limelight much after his death. They say he correctly predicted the world wars and assassinations of a few famous personalities!"

"Oh yes! He is the master of prophecies," said Laila. "Nobody has correctly predicted so many global events like him. It's so unreal. But, mind you, he was an astrologer and not a tarot reader."

"Young man, I also have something interesting to tell you. The three of you are special people born with a purpose on this earth, and your lives are going to change drastically in a little while. Just wait and watch."

"Everyone is special and everyone comes with a purpose in life. What is so great about us?" questioned Tony.

"Right now, you may not believe in what I said but you will realize it later. All I can say is that after you leave Goa, your lives will not be the same. Here is my card, whenever you feel that there was some truth in my words, please call me."

"Hey Krish, what's that book you are reading?" Asif asked.

"Man, why are you shouting? Please pull out your headphones and then speak!"

"No, leave it. You carry on with your book," winked Asif. Such was his love for music that he would first put on his headphone even before fastening his seat belt.

They had no idea about Tony's discussion with the Tarot lady.

* * *

"John, have you noticed people on a flight?"

"The first thing they do after boarding can tell you a lot about them. The studious ones will start with the magazines and finish with the travel manual. Music lovers will put on their headphones before anything else and the dreamers zone out to their imaginary worlds, gazing out of the window and admiring the never-ending sky and beautiful clouds."

"What would you say about me Yogi? I love to play my mobile games the moment I am buckled up in my seat," John said, bringing the focus on to himself.

"Ha ha. John you are one of the best publishers in America, but I must say that you have a boy inside you who is always peeping out of your grey hair and crow's feet. To tell you the truth my friend, that's how we are supposed to live, a child is always cheerful in all situations."

"Coming back to our story, life is full of surprises and the trio did not have the slightest hint about what was going to happen. All they knew was that Goa was the place for them and all they wanted was to live in that moment."

* * *

"Wake up, Asif, the plane is about to land," said Krish tapping his shoulder.

"Oh! I didn't realize! I just fell asleep listening to the music," said Asif, rubbing his eyes.

Tony and Laila, all this while, had some interesting discussions on history, astrology, and all possible subjects one could think of.

Everyone was excited to step on to the land of vices and couldn't wait to get out of the plane. The usual security formalities seemed so long and tedious.

The eyes of this trio were eagerly waiting to see the glitz and glamour the city had to offer. They hurried through the airport formalities and hired a cab to the hotel.

The driver was instructed to take them through the city centre even if it meant taking a longer route.

"Could you suggest some good places for us to visit?" Tony asked the cab driver.

"Goa is full of good places, sir! But I would certainly recommend the 'must see' ones. That's what I love about my job," said the driver, looking into the rear-view mirror.

"I would suggest you go to Fire on Ice. It is indeed one of the finest pubs in Goa with the best crowd you would want to meet."

"Since you are in Goa, you must surely try your hands at gambling. Play only for fun or you will end up losing all you have," warned the cab driver.

"In the end, only the casinos make money. I have seen people losing all their money and not having enough to buy air tickets back to their hometowns."

The driver was a local, a strongly built middle aged man with tattoos all over his arms, neck, and knuckles. One could easily mistake him for a drug-dealing Columbian fugitive but his polite tone and friendly behaviour showed that he had spent all his life on the city roads.

He was very patient in answering all their queries and dropped them in front of the hotel within thirty minutes.

They thoroughly enjoyed the ride and, quite pleased, rewarded him with a hefty tip.

The hotel was a newly constructed mid-sized one with a huge lobby. The designer had indeed done a beautiful job with classic chandeliers, landscape paintings everywhere, shiny wooden flooring and a majestic swimming pool.

They quickly checked into their respective rooms and decided to meet exactly in half an hour in the hotel lobby.

Like always, Krish was the first one to get ready and reach the lobby. Since he reached before time, he went to the lobby manager and asked, "Could you please suggest some good place for dinner?"

"Sir, this is a city of fun and food. You would find good restaurants all over," the lobby manager wittily replied.

"I know, that's what the cab driver also said but still, any favourites?"

"Sir, it depends on the kind of food you would like to have. There is a nice Thai restaurant in the next block, you may try it if you wish to have Thai delicacies tonight."

"Please get ready soon and meet me in the lobby," said Asif, knocking on Tony's door.

It was eight p.m. when they all stepped out of the hotel. Though hungry as hell, they wanted to find an excellent restaurant.

They wanted to try all sorts of exotic dishes but started off with the Thai restaurant as suggested by the lobby manager. It was just one block away from the hotel, well decorated with Thai paintings and dim lights. The traditional lamp shades gave it a classy, oriental look.

It was going to be a long night for them and after having a few drinks and enough snacks, they stepped out of the restaurant in search of an exotic pub.

The streets were all aglitter and there were big hotels all over, with neon lights and huge bill boards. The hustle and bustle of this place was matchless.

A place for pure indulgence where one could find the crème de la crème of the world flaunting their riches.

"Shall we go to Fire on Ice?" asked Tony. "That cab driver said it was near our hotel."

"I hope it actually is good. What would a cab driver know about pubs?" Krish opined.

"Don't say that, bro. That's what they do, day in and day out. When it comes to knowing the most authentic places—the local drivers, my friend, can easily beat all the Lonely Planets of the world," said Asif.

Well, Fire on Ice was real fun; it exceeded their expectations. After having a few drinks, they danced to the fabulous music. They were also surrounded by beautiful women.

Only when the bartender asked them to order their last drinks did they realize that it was almost four in the morning and time for them to go back to their hotel.

"Good morning, friends!" Asif said mockingly, stepping out of the pub.

"C'mon guys, we are here for fun and four o'clock is just late night," winked Tony. "We don't have our families waiting for us."

"Thank God Mira isn't waiting for me at the hotel or this would have been the last day of my life," Krish said laughingly.

"Man! I'm so glad to be single. You married people have no life of your own," said Asif.

"I second that," said Tony, with a naughty smile on his face.

"Don't worry, you both will also face that music someday," said Krish.

It was almost sunrise when they reached the hotel, went to their respective rooms, and fell on their beds.

The next day was reserved for recreational activities.

They woke up in the afternoon, obviously skipped breakfast, got ready and left for the theme park for an adrenalin rush.

Krish warned both of them, "Please don't force me to try the roller coaster ride. I am a married man and have my wife and two children to look after."

"C'mon Krish, you aren't going to die on it. These people have an impeccable record. Nobody ever fell from any of those rides. You are a rich man with a big insurance cover so don't worry about the family," said Tony with the most serious expression. He had this knack of confusing people by cracking jokes with a serious face.

"Thanks, Tony! With friends like you who needs enemies?" said Krish.

Asif giggled, "C'mon bro, Tony is just trying to motivate you, and truth be told, life itself is a roller coaster ride."

"Oh really?" replied Krish with a raised eyebrow. "I am impressed with his motivational skills. In fact, he should write a book on motivation."

After two hours of fun at the theme park, they had lunch and went back to the hotel to take a nap and be fresh for the evening.

The evening started with drinks at the hotel bar itself.

After a few drinks Asif said, "Let's go to the casino. But remember one thing—we are going there just for fun and not to make a fortune so do not get carried away if you win a game or two."

To which everyone echoed a resounding 'yes.'

They had never seen something like this before. The casino was like a huge five-star hotel with beautiful hostesses and croupiers with Greek God looks and English mannerisms. This was the place where thousands of people lost millions and a lucky handful made their fortunes.

"My Gosh! Look at the hostesses here; they are so gorgeous. I can spend the whole night gazing at them," murmured Asif with his eyes popping out.

"Welcome to Goa," said Tony.

"Hey guys! Let's go to different tables and meet here in half an hour," Krish suggested.

"Yes, and then we can share our experiences," echoed Tony.

"And whoever wins will treat the others to dinner," said an excited Asif.

It was their first gambling experience and thankfully they had already been warned that the only guaranteed winner was the casino.

Having placed small bets and losing whatever little money they had allocated for gambling, they thought of going back to the pub as losing money on drinks was a better idea than losing it to gambling.

A few more drinks down the hatch and Asif wanted to go to watch pole dancing. "Who wants to see the famous La Vida pole dance of Goa?"

Tony was the first one to raise his hand. "I have heard so much about that place," said Tony. "I hope I won't be disappointed tonight."

"Are you kidding me? People from all over the world come here to see it. A cousin of mine who once visited Goa told me not to miss the pole dancing at La Vida," said Asif.

"Well, I too read in some travel magazine about Goa. But honestly I am not too keen on visiting this place," said Krish with visible disappointment on his face.

"Are you crazy? You are in Goa and refuse to see the world-famous pole dance here?" Tony asked incredulously.

"Well! Yes and no. I want to see it for fun but if I see it my heart will be filled with guilt," replied a downcast Krish.

"How will Mira react if she knows I visited this place?"

"You've got to be kidding man," said Asif.

"Coming all the way to Goa and not seeing those beauties will be suicidal. Please save your guilt for something else. Just pretend that you didn't see it and if your heart is still complaining, put the blame on us. Also remember, 'what happens in Goa, remains in Goa'!" said Tony and started laughing.

"Ok! I'm coming," said Krish. "But if my family comes to know about it, I will tell them you forced me."

What a place La Vida was! It was indeed one of the best live entertainments they had ever seen. Such gorgeous dancers with their hourglass figures could bring even the noblest of men to their knees.

The next three days were spent pub hopping, drinking, and dancing, and after many days of alcohol and women, they finally ran out of steam.

***

"Yogi, do you believe in astrology? Is it a science or an art?"

"Well John, yes, I am a firm believer in astrology and I think that it is more of a science."

"Are you serious? How can a planet which is more than a million kilometres away impact my thoughts or behaviour? And why would you link it to science?"

"Let me try to make it simple for you, John. The very basis of astrology is the movement of planets at a given time and their effect on human beings."

"Answer this? Do you agree that all human beings are made of matter?"

"Beyond any doubt. How can I not believe what science tells us?" I was holding my fort.

"Great, similarly science also tells us that all the planets, stars, moons, asteroids, etc. are also made of matter. Which means everything in the universe has the same basic ingredients. Right?"

"Ahem! You can say that, Yogi."

"Now let me ask you a question, John. Who has influenced you the most since your childhood?"

"Well, there are many of them. But to start with, my father has been my biggest inspiration, followed by Musk for my love of science, and then Branson, the media baron."

"Thank you, John. As per your reasoning about distance, the only person who could have influenced you should have been your father as he is biologically connected and is closest to you, unlike the other two you mentioned."

"Son, distance is only in the mind and that is why you were equally influenced by a person living more than 6,000 kilometres away from you. Hold on to your thoughts now."

"I can say this with full confidence that someone else belonging to a similar background like yours may have different influencers in life."

"The entire Universe is one and we all are like packets of energy. Our forms and shapes decide the roles we play in the grand design."

"Our Universe is a very dynamic, and a continuously evolving place. Since the planets revolve around the Sun in an elliptical manner, their distance from Earth varies at different times, and their effect at different positions becomes our time. Holistically speaking, we are all made of the same matter and thus affect each other, but the intensity may depend on the distance and time."

"I don't wish to sound corny, but how does a tsunami in Japan killing hundreds of people affect us? We have no direct connection with those people in Japan."

"Now, talking about effect of astronomical bodies on human beings, let us start with our closest neighbour. It is a well-known fact that a full moon's gravitational pull creates high tides on earth. It also has an adverse effect on the minds of some people, and that is where the term 'lunatic' came from."

"Let's go one step further. Some astronomers believe that the Moon was once a part of our Earth. As per this theory, some microorganisms on Earth that became fossils over millions of years may be a part of our Moon now. Even we may become a part of another planet millions of years from now."

"Yogi, that is too much science for me but your metaphor has kind of answered my queries. I may not start believing in it but I definitely wish to explore it further."

Chapter 3

A beautiful, sunny day was happily spent inside a shopping mall. After all, these were the last few moments of the trip and in a few hours, everyone would go back to their daily routines. Goa was indeed going to be missed—the week seemed to have flown by in a few hours.

As decided, the three friends met around two p.m. in the hotel lobby and hired a cab. They reached the airport in thirty minutes. Unlike Mumbai airport, there were no long queues.

The sky was clear and the flight was full. The pretty cabin crew received the full attention of the passengers while giving their routine instructions.

The flight took off smoothly, and the flight attendants had already started offering snacks and drinks to the passengers. The flight being just an hour and a half long, the hostesses were in a hurry.

Suddenly, a woman from the front row started yelling, drawing everyone's attention. A scary sight indeed—a man was holding a gun to her head and threatening to kill her.

"I am Jack and this flight has been hijacked!" said the man with a wicked smile. He was tall with cold, blue eyes and a trimmed beard. "I am sure you all had fun in Goa. Its time I show you a different type of entertainment. Any guesses? Anyone?"

"How about you miss, can you tell me what I am going to do next?" asked the hijacker to the woman he held hostage, and started laughing madly.

"I promise, I will not shoot any passengers. I will only kill both the pilots of this plane and then we will all see the plane nose dive from 25,000 feet, crash into the sea and in the next fifteen minutes, we all will be in heaven. It's live entertainment and it's free. Interesting, yeah?" He again started laughing like the psychopath he was.

"But why do you want to kill us?" asked one of the passengers in a strained voice.

"Good question! I have always dreamt of an eventful life but never had one. So, I decided to have an eventful death. Nothing excites me like dying in a plane crash. And now, you all should pray to your Gods!" he screamed.

"Tell us what your demands are," intervened the flight purser. "We can send your message across."

"Please take all our money but don't kill us," pleaded another passenger.

"I don't need your money," said the hijacker in an angry voice. "I just want this plane to crash. Hijacking a plane would make enough noise and I will become famous even after my death." He was laughing again.

By now everyone had realized that their lives were in danger, unsure if they would ever see their families again.

"Oh, Jesus, I don't want to die so young, we all had such an amazing trip. Is it going to end up like this? Is this the turnaround event that Laila was referring to?" Tony was crying like a child.

"Calm down, Tony! Have faith in God, I am sure we will survive this," said Krish, holding his hand firmly.

"See how Asif is controlling his nerves."

"Talking about Laila, remember, she spoke about us doing something different for society. If we die today, the only contribution will be our ashes," said Krish teasingly, trying to calm his friend, though he was equally disturbed by the situation.

There were howling sounds everywhere.

"Man, this is no time to joke," said Tony. He was scared to death and had given up all hope.

The pilot appealed to all the passengers to calm down and requested the hijacker to talk things over amicably. But the hijacker was in no mood for negotiations and wouldn't hesitate to kill someone.

The constant fear of death was gnawing at them. They say seeing death so near tiggers flashbacks—thinking about their families and how much they would miss them. Repenting for not being able to spend much time with their loved ones.

Suddenly, two men sitting behind the captured lady pounced on the hijacker. They snatched away his gun and took him into custody. Those God-sent angels were retired cops who were working as security officers at a hotel in Goa.

All the passengers applauded their bravery and cursed the hijacker. In a matter of a few minutes their lives had changed. Now, everyone was thanking their good fortune, looking forward to landing safely and rushing home to their families.

"Thank God! I want to reach Mumbai as soon as possible," said Tony taking a deep breath.

"Yes indeed! Before something else happens," said Asif. He finally had a reason to show his teeth.

"Do you people trust me now? I told you both, we shall survive," said Krish with a smile. "We must thank God for saving our lives. We have been given a second chance and hence, we need to do some very serious thinking about our future."

"You are so right," said both Asif and Tony in unison.

Chapter 4

With tears in his eyes, Asif narrated the whole story to his family who were deeply shocked and thanked God that their son and his friends had returned unhurt.

They say, only in the dark can you see the stars. Asif was a changed man now. He promised his father that he would take up a job soon and also offer his daily prayers.

"We came unscathed from the clutches of death. Thought I would never see you again, Dad," said Tony teary eyed as he gave his father another tight hug.

His father too was startled to hear about the dramatic end to their fun-filled trip.

Indeed, a moment of awakening, Tony too realized that life is nothing without a purpose.

Krish's family had no clue about his experiences on the Goa trip, nor did he want to discuss it on a long-distance call.

Surviving a plane hijack had reaffirmed his belief in destiny and also triggered his quest for spirituality. Suddenly a highly successful career, money, luxury, etc. appeared to be useless.

A quick telephone call the next morning, and everyone agreed to meet at the park in the evening.

The happy-go-lucky boys had returned as sober men.

The basketball court that evening appeared like an amphitheatre. This was probably the first time Asif was a spectator sitting outside the court.

"This is the beauty of life," Krish broke the silence.

"A fun filled trip to Goa ended like that and suddenly everything seems so worthless."

"Couldn't agree more! Money can buy you almost everything but not your life. Especially if you are stuck with a money hating psychopathic killer."

"Lesson learned! I am planning to take up a sales job in an auto store," Asif said, taking a deep breath.

"Wow! That sounds great. You have always been fond of cars," said Krish.

"I am so happy for you," said Tony patting Asif's shoulder.

"Guys, we should be thankful to the Almighty for opening our eyes," said Krish.

"Agreed!" said both Asif and Tony.

Ironically, a trip to one of the most materialistic places in the world had turned into a spiritual experience for the three of them.

Asif was seemingly moved the most. He started working seriously, shunned alcohol and became a puritan.

Krish had always been a spiritual person. But now he desperately needed a bigger, stronger dose of it.

Weeks passed and life went back to being normal.

Tony and Krish did meet a couple of times but Asif's presence was dearly missed.

Too focused on his job, Asif would leave early in the morning everyday only to come back late at night. He didn't socialize much, the weekdays were spent at his work place and the weekends were reserved for community work.

* * *

"John, it looks like we are near Moradabad! Our first halt."

"How can you tell, Yogi? All I can see is farms on both sides."

"Didn't you notice the hoardings of 'Contact for World's Best Brass' in the corner of those sugarcane farms? That's Moradabad for you, my friend. The City of Brass!"

"Oh! That's interesting."

"Yes, and equally interesting is the history of the Mughal prince, Murad Baksh. Apparently, the city was named after him."

"This is a classic example of the law of karmic return. Do you wish to hear a bit of history?"

"Why not, Yogi? To me, history is as important as predicting the future."

"Good to hear that. So, when the Emperor Shah Jahan grew old and fragile, two of his sons Dara Shikoh and Aurangzeb declared themselves as emperors."

"Murad, the youngest of them all, stood by Aurangzeb and helped him in killing Dara and imprisoning their father, Shah Jahan."

"But when Aurangzeb became the emperor, he imprisoned Murad and didn't think twice before executing him."

"Soup, sir!" The intense discussion on Mughal history was interrupted by the cabin attendant.

"These Rajdhani chaps keep your mouth busy all through the journey," said Yogi with a chuckle.

I did not utter a single word. I wanted Yogi to continue the story.

Chapter 5

One day, while surfing through his television channels, Tony saw the news of some Tibetan monks visiting Mumbai for a spiritual discourse.

Buddhism was indeed his favourite subject and the mere idea of interacting with the monks made him excited. His wish to meet his old forgotten friend and spiritual guru was rekindled.

All these years, he had been following the teachings of Dorjee, and in his moments of trouble, he remembered the monk's cool and calm face and drew strength from it.

"Hey man, I have something to tell you," said Tony as he picked up the phone and called Krish.

"What is it? Tell me quickly." Krish was equally enthused.

"Something really interesting to share. I can't tell you on the phone. Can we please meet this evening?" urged Tony.

"Sure! How about seven p.m., my place?" Krish could sense Tony's excitement and didn't want to disappoint him.

"Sounds good," said Tony and hung up.

The doorbell rang at seven sharp that evening, two continuous rings meant that someone was in a real hurry.

"Come on in, Tony. Please have a seat. What can I offer you?" said Krish playing the perfect host.

"A cup of coffee would be great," said Tony.

The coffee was already brewing as Krish didn't want to waste time in the kitchen.

"So, you wanted to tell me something, Tony?"

"Oh yes, I have something very interesting to tell you," Tony said, taking the first sip of the freshly brewed coffee.

"You won't believe what I saw on TV today. There is a delegation of Buddhist monks visiting downtown for a spiritual discourse. I am so very excited about it," said Tony, wriggling on the couch.

"Are you for real? Is this what you couldn't discuss with me on the phone?"

"What's the big deal about monks visiting Mumbai? I am sure there are hundreds of them visiting every year."

"My friend, I know that. But this one is special. This delegation is from Dharamshala. Do you remember that Tibetan Buddhist friend of mine?"

"No! I don't, as you never did tell me about him," said Krish.

"Oh! Then I must have shared it with Asif."

"Actually, I met a monk named Dorjee, through a common friend back when I was in school. I was so impressed with him that I ended up making him my spiritual guru," said Tony.

"Oh! But why did you choose him as your guru? What was so special about him?" asked Krish, surprised.

"Well, he was the one who introduced me to Buddhism

and enticed me towards the world of spirituality. I still practice the sacred chants he gave me."

"Oh really! Sounds interesting," said Krish. "And where is he now? Dharamshala?"

"Guess he is in Tibet but I haven't heard from him in ages," said Tony with a huge sigh.

"Today, when I saw this news about some Tibetan monks visiting Mumbai, I got so excited. I wondered if this is my chance at finding my long-lost friend. Krish, I urge you to join me in attending these discourses."

"They may know the whereabouts of Dorjee and even if they don't, listening to those enlightened souls is always a blissful experience," said Tony. He already knew the answer Krish would give.

"You are right, my friend. Buddhist monks are quite spiritual and are at absolute peace with themselves. There is a lot one can learn from them. By the way, have I ever told you about my Buddhist connection?"

"Not really!"

"Well, there was this Buddhist monastery and a few of the monks from there were friends of mine. We used to play football in the evenings," said Krish in a nostalgic tone.

"Actually, I was born in a small village called Sarnath. This is the place where Lord Buddha gave his first sermon."

"It is just ten kilometres from Varanasi, and is one of the oldest cities in the world. It's a very sacred place for us Hindus and that's where my family lives these days."

"It's indeed a very special place, with an interesting mix of both Hindus and Buddhist populations living peacefully. However, you may often come across confused intellectuals attempting to intertwine both these beliefs."

"Sounds interesting," said Tony. "Now you have all the more reason to accompany me."

"Sorry, my friend, I would love to, but right now for me, time is of the essence. I have a few very important meetings lined up in the next few days."

"Well, we have time till Monday evening and I will go just for a couple of hours," said Tony. "Please do come along with me Krish," Tony pleaded.

"Alright, let's do it. You never really give me a choice," smiled Krish. "But mind you, only two hours."

"You are indeed my true friend," said Tony with a happy smile.

The prayer hall was well decorated with beautiful Tibetan paintings of Lord Buddha. It depicted the different stages of his life that talked about his journey from his birth till he attained *Nirvana*.

Managing to reach the monastery before time, they both grabbed the front seats.

The place felt so magnificent, filled with the sweet smell of incense. The resonating sound of "*Om Mani Padme Hum*," the Buddhist chant, was a treat to the ears and solace to the mind.

This rejuvenating aura gave one the feeling of being in some ancient monastery in the midst of the Himalayas.

Then came the moment which everyone had eagerly been waiting for. Everyone stood and greeted the religious leaders with a huge round of applause.

Interestingly, the discourse started with Buddhism but then moved on to different issues that the world was facing, including terrorism, global warming, etc.

Although that's not what you expect in a spiritual discourse, unfortunately, in today's world, it's difficult to decouple religion from politics.

The monks managed to very politely answer the questions posed by the audience about their beliefs, differences, and similarities with other religions. Even a nonspiritual subject like freedom of practicing religion in Tibet, etc.

A meaningful and interesting discourse was subtly ended by one of the monks. They had crossed the stipulated time and had to wrap up the discourse there.

"Thanks, Tony," said Krish as they left the hall.

"Thanks for what?"

"For forcing me to come here," answered Krish. He was indeed overwhelmed.

"Ha! I knew you would like it here," said Tony with a sense of pride.

During the tea break, Tony asked the other monks if they knew the whereabouts of Dorjee but none of them had any clue. With more than fifty monasteries in Tibet it was impossible for them to know all the monks.

Although disheartened, Tony's desire to meet Dorjee grew stronger.

Whilst listening to the discourse, he even thought of travelling to Dharamshala to look for his spiritual guru.

"Hey Krish, I was wondering if I should make a trip to Dharamshala to find my long lost friend. I could enrol myself in a Buddhism course too."

"Terrific idea, but I hope I am not a part of your plan this time. Before you say anything, let me tell you I am leaving for Varanasi in a couple of weeks."

"You are such a genius, Krish! How did you know that I am planning to take you along?" said Tony pulling his cheeks and teasing him.

"Tony, I am not kidding," replied Krish, attempting to defy the proposal.

"Neither am I," Tony replied confidently. As if he knew that Krish would eventually agree to his plan.

"Ok. Here is the deal. You have to reach Varanasi in two weeks, right?"

"Yes," said Krish.

"So, we will go to Dharamshala first and from there you can fly to Varanasi. I promise I won't force you to stay for more than a week. You will see a new place and learn a bit more about Buddhism. Not to mention the fun that you always have while you are with me," Tony said with a deadpan look on his face.

"Thanks for the offer, 'Mr King of Good Times'," winked Krish. "I will positively think about it and even if I decide to join you, it will only be for a few days. Okay?"

"What would I do without you, Krish?" said Tony with

a naughty smile on his face. "But there is a problem. My father. It will be hard to convince him."

"Uncle? Why would he stop you from going there?"

"My father has never stepped out of Mumbai. He firmly believes that other than his own city, the entire world is unsafe."

"But he trusts you. So if I tell him that Krish is accompanying me, he will have no problem with it."

"Alright, I will come tomorrow and talk to your father. Let's see what he has to say. May I go home now with His Majesty's permission?" said Krish with a mock salute.

"Ha ha! Yes, you may," replied Tony.

The next morning, Krish showed up at Tony's house.

"Hello, Uncle! How are you?" Krish extended his arm for a hand shake.

"I am good son. Long time no see," said Tony's father as he stood up and gave him a warm hug.

"Sorry uncle, I have been very busy with work lately."

"Tony, please go and get some coffee for Krish," his father requested. "Heard you guys had an eventful time on your trip to Goa. Tell me about it. It's entertainment of all sorts!"

"Sounds like Elizabeth Gilbert's unwritten book, 'Food-Drinks-Fear.' I must say, Tony is a changed man now. He is focused on store sales and spends a good amount of time at home too. The Goa trip has certainly done a great deal of good for him, you should do more of these trips," said Tony's father with an 'I know it all' smile.

"By the way, how's your family in Varanasi? Aren't you going there soon?"

"Oh! They are all well, uncle, thank you. I will be joining them in a couple of weeks. In fact, I wanted to speak to you about that," said Krish.

"What? You need my permission to go to Varanasi now? Ha ha. That's funny!"

"Actually, Tony and I are planning to go to the mountains for some time and from there I shall proceed to my hometown. We wanted to seek your permission for this trip," said Krish in a sheepish tone.

"A trip to the Himalayas? Why on earth would you want to visit that Godforsaken place? To meet Shamans?" Tony's father asked in a reproving tone. His smile was all gone now.

"To tell you the truth, Tony wants to meet his friend Dorjee in Dharamshala and we both want to study a bit of Buddhism. All this will be in the backdrop of the mighty Himalayas."

"You need not worry about Tony. I will take care of him," said Krish. His convincing tone had already done the trick.

"Honestly, I am not too comfortable sending Tony out of Mumbai; he has never travelled beyond Goa. But since you are accompanying him, I have no second thoughts," said Tony's father.

In the meantime, Tony came in with the coffee and placed it on the table.

"Tony, I will agree to this trip only if you promise that you will not try to be too adventurous and will write to me about your well-being at least once a week," said his father with a huge sigh.

"Thank you so much, dad," said Tony hugging his father.

"Don't worry, he will write to you regularly from there," said Krish as he got up to leave.

"Hey man, finish your coffee before you leave," said Tony.

"No dude. I just remembered some urgent work I need to finish before our trip. See you at the airport!"

***

"Sorry to interrupt you, Yogi! Just a random thought. How is it that Buddhism spread all over the world from India but is almost non-existent in the country of its birth?"

"That's an interesting observation, John. I shall try to answer it. Firstly, Lord Buddha is one of India's greatest saints and Buddhism today is respected by a vast majority of Indians. However, let me try to give you some perspective."

"John, you are a successful publisher. You recruit an intern, train him well, share all your knowledge and experience with him. And one day that same recruit grows through the ranks and eventually becomes a threat to your business. Who is at fault here?"

"Is it John who, with all honesty and dedication, imparted all his knowledge to this youngster, fulfilling his duty as a supervisor? Or is it the fast learning, suave, and intelligent young professional who unknowingly became a threat to his seniors?"

"Well, I think no one is at fault here. Both were doing their jobs," said a rather confident John.

"You are right! And I hope you took it in the right context."

"Although Buddha was born in Nepal, he became Lord Buddha only after attaining enlightenment under the Bodhi tree in India, gave his first sermon at Sarnath. He then travelled all over teaching the 'Four Noble Truths' and the 'Noble Eight-fold Path.'"

"In the next 200 years, Buddhism spread all over India, South and Central Asia because of the great Mauryan King, Asoka."

"If it wasn't for the Sunga King Pushyamitra, this country would have been different today. I am not saying it is right or wrong, and like you rightly said, no one is at fault. That's destiny for you."

"Like us humans, nations too have their destiny. Written sometimes by the sword and at other times by the saints.

"Now, would you like to take a tea break? Or shall we move back to my story?" Yogi asked.

"Certainly! A cup of tea would be great."

I was still trying to make sense of it all.

Chapter 6

The flights from Mumbai to New Delhi and further to Dharamshala were pretty tiring.

Tony and Krish went to the monastery in Dharamshala, where they were told that Dorjee had moved to Lhasa. Tony was disheartened but Krish persuaded him to make the short trip to Tibet. Although they were totally exhausted, they drove back to the Delhi airport that very evening.

Tibet was an enchanting place, nested in the Northern Himalayas and aptly called 'The roof of the world.'

Tony and Krish were extremely excited about the trip.

Till now, Tony had only heard stories about the charisma of the mountain ranges. He kept wondering how life would be in those beautiful snowcapped mountains.

Unfortunately for him, the window seat was of no use, as his desire for an aerial view remained unfulfilled. There was a thick layer of clouds covering the Himalayan ranges and one could barely see the glaciers.

The wait was finally over and the flight landed at Lhasa airport which was an hour's drive from the city centre. A bit small for an airport, but an efficiently managed one.

Lhasa was a beautiful valley surrounded by snowcapped mountains, supposedly the birth place of Tibetan Buddhism.

Ironically, Lord Buddha had never travelled to this part of the world in his lifetime, yet it was the torch bearer of modern Buddhism.

Having collected their luggage and finished formalities at customs, the duo hired a cab and went directly to the hotel booked by their travel agent.

"I am feeling a bit nauseous," said Tony the moment they stepped out of the airport.

"Welcome to Tibet," smiled Krish. "My friend, right now we are in a city located on one of the highest altitudes in the world and due to that, oxygen availability is low."

"Aren't you feeling the same?" Tony curiously asked.

"Yes, I am," nodded Krish. "Anybody traveling for the first time to this part of the world would take at least a day or two to get used to this altitude."

"I can now imagine the problem mountaineers face while trying to climb Mount Everest," said Tony with childlike wonder.

"Well, Everest is a different ordeal, we are talking about scaling the world's highest point. That's why they have camps at different levels to acclimatize themselves."

"Actually, dearth of oxygen is only one of the challenges that climbers face. Imagine, you are just 500 meters from reaching glory and suddenly there is a blizzard. You have only two options—either you risk your life and go for the summit or climb down to the nearest base camp and start afresh," Krish explained.

"Talking about Tibet, you know, Tony, it's winter and definitely not the best time to visit!" he continued.

"But Krish, I couldn't have waited till summer, and even you didn't have much to do because you are going home for a holiday." Tony defended his decision.

The drive to the hotel was quite picturesque as the cab cruised through the beautiful mountain terrain. Reaching the hotel in just about half an hour, both of them quickly checked in and rushed to their rooms to freshen up.

"Hey, are you ready for dinner?" asked Krish, knocking on Tony's door.

"Half an hour!" shouted Tony from inside.

"Ok. Let's meet in the lobby," Krish shouted back and left.

"So, what shall we have for dinner tonight?" asked Tony as he joined Krish at the lobby.

"First tell me, why do you take so long to get ready? Even Cleopatra wouldn't be spending so much time in the bathtub," said Krish sarcastically.

"Oh c'mon, I didn't take that long. It was just forty-five minutes, and by the way, Nefertiti would be a better comparison for me...huh! Can we please talk about dinner now," said Tony sounding a bit irritated, as shower time was a very personal matter to him.

"Hey, since we are both exhausted, shall we have dinner in the hotel's restaurant itself? I heard they have a nice Tibetan menu," said Krish.

"Fine by me," Tony agreed.

Too tired to relish the food, they ordered the dishes on the basis of the time it would take for them to be prepared. Quickly finishing dinner, both went off to their rooms.

It was a perfect starlit night—the stubborn clouds were chased away by the wind flowing down the mountains.

Lying in bed, Tony was quietly looking out the window. For him, this was an altogether different world. He could not recall the last time he had seen so many stars. It was a long, chilly night indeed, and thankfully, the hotel rooms were warm enough. The two friends woke up the next morning to the sweet sound of ringing bells and chanting from the nearby monastery.

What a perfect way to start a bright, sunny day! The duo had their morning tea followed by a walk in the well-maintained hotel garden. The property was on a cliff and the surrounding view was beyond breathtaking.

"Let's get ready and meet at the lobby in an hour," said Krish.

"You are right my friend. Let's not waste any more time, we are here on a mission," replied Tony as he too rushed back to his room.

Having quickly finished their breakfast, they decided to start their search for Dorjee at the most famous Drepung monastery.

Knowing well that Tony would take extra time to get ready, Krish utilized his spare time gathering information about the monasteries, as there were quite a few in Lhasa.

Searching for Dorjee among the thousands of monks was going to be a daunting task but Tony was unperturbed and determined to find his long-lost friend and mentor.

The Drepung monastery was the biggest and arguably the best in Tibet. Young monks from all over the country would come to study here and then go back to their native places, spending their lives in the service of Buddhism.

"Jeez! How are we going to find your friend? With their shaven heads and those yellow robes, they all look alike," moaned Krish, pointing to the monks in the monastery.

"You are right, Krish, but guess what? It was only those yellow robes that first attracted me to Dorjee when I saw him in Mumbai," said Tony.

"If I am not mistaken, there are a few Europeans monks here too," said Krish.

"C'mon, how do you know that the Caucasian-looking monks are from Europe? You haven't yet spoken to them. They could be from North America," argued Tony.

"Well, I can tell by my experience, not many Americans would have heard about Tibet, and the ones who know would prefer visiting Alaska if they wanted to see snowcapped mountains," Krish noted with a smile on his face.

"You are right, brother! Americans waste most of their life in the rat race. Where is the time to explore the world?" Tony smirked.

"Don't you think it would be better if we go to that prayer hall and meditate a bit before starting our search?" Krish interrupted as he wanted to bring the focus back to the task at hand.

"Sure, that will be a great way to start," said Tony in an excited whisper and they both walked towards the prayer hall.

Having spent some quiet moments in front of the huge bronze statue of Lord Buddha, they started talking to other monks. As expected, most of them could not speak English. Now the challenge was to find an Anglophonic monk.

They finally managed to get hold of a French monk. Unfortunately for them, he could barely speak English.

"He wouldn't have helped us even if he could speak English," said Krish.

"Why do you say so?" quizzed Tony. "I had a French neighbour and he wasn't that bad."

"Well, it is because of their history. France and England fought so many wars against each other and the French were mostly on the losing side. Their history still haunts them and apparently a majority of the French don't think highly of the English, be it the language or the people," elucidated Krish.

"That's strange and interesting to know considering they fought the Second World War as allies," laughed Tony.

After half an hour of searching they finally came across a Chinese monk, Hu Xing who could speak a little English.

When asked about Dorjee, Hu Xing replied that he didn't know many monks as he had recently moved from a different city, but he could introduce them to someone at the Tibetan Buddhist council who would surely be able to help them. The meeting could only be organized after two days as the monk who could help had gone to a different city.

"I think it makes sense. Trying to find Dorjee through a council member would be sensible," said Krish.

"You are right. Let's wait for him to arrive and in the meantime, we could do some sightseeing. What say?" asked Tony feeling proud of his proposal. This was their only option though.

"Makes sense," replied Krish as they both thanked Hu Xing and left the monastery.

"Hang on, Krish! Did you ask for the contact details of that monk?" Tony questioned urgently.

"No, I didn't," replied Krish in a very innocent tone.

"Gosh! How are we going to find him after two days?" said Tony.

"Why do we have to ask his whereabouts, Tony? He is a monk, right?" said Krish.

"Yes," affirmed Tony.

"The monks are supposed to live in monasteries, we know his name and that's enough. Now let's go out and explore Lhasa. You are such a gimp!" continued Krish tapping his head.

"Sure," replied Tony in a sheepish tone.

The rest of the day was spent in recreational activities, special Kung Fu shows, exploring the local market and the city zoo, with its biggest attraction being a recently caught snow leopard.

"It's such a pity that this beautiful animal is under threat of extinction," said Krish pointing to the snow leopard.

"Considering the Tibetans' fondness for their claws and teeth, I would be worried about this one too," said Tony sardonically as they headed towards the market.

Shopping was not really on their agenda as most of the shops were selling the same Chinese goods that all world markets were flooded with.

The evening was spent inside the monastery, surfing books in the library and interacting with other monks.

Tony often wondered how Buddhism had managed to become one of the most widely spread religions in the world so peacefully. It does not actively encourage religious conversions yet so many people all over the world embrace it.

Perhaps the most compelling reason was their inherent message of peace and harmony. Yet, there were so many questions left unanswered and Tony knew that only Dorjee would be able to answer them.

It was getting dark and with many thoughts in their minds, they left for the hotel. Midway, they stopped at a restaurant for dinner; it was a good opportunity to try some local delicacies.

"The food was delicious," said a clearly delighted Tony. He seemed to enjoy anything that was Tibetan.

"You are right Tony. Their food is indeed rich and tasty."

"Nothing like having a sumptuous meal and sleeping long hours," said Tony.

"Well, unfortunately, tomorrow we don't have the option of waking up late," replied Krish.

"But why?"

"The lobby manager of our hotel told me not to miss the first rays of the sun and that the Himalayan sunrise is something to die for," said Krish.

"I don't remember the last time I saw a sunrise," Tony said.

"Well, this is your opportunity and I insist you get up early tomorrow morning," said Krish. He didn't want both of them to miss that spectacular view.

Like a painter's imagination, the magnificent sunrays were lighting up the peaks of the snow-clad mountains. The duo thoroughly enjoyed the view and thanked God for giving them the opportunity to visit this beautiful Himalayan abode.

After sipping a hot cup of tea on the terrace, they went to their rooms to freshen up and go out to the market. This was probably their last day for sightseeing as the next day they would be going to meet the council man to find out the whereabouts of Dorjee.

It was a day well spent; Krish and Tony went back to the monastery and made new friends. Then they also went to the nearby lake and spent almost the whole day there, returning to their rooms only at night.

The next morning, they reached the monastery at half past 8 and went directly to the prayer hall.

Surprisingly, Hu was already there, waiting for them. He served them a special tea along with dim sums and then they left for the Buddhist council which was in the city centre.

Tony, Krish, and Hu Xing were greeted by Norbu, a gray-haired man with a wrinkled face who was waiting for them at the main gate.

He was very polite and soft spoken.

"So, what brings you to Lhasa?" asked Norbu as he shook hands with them one by one.

"Sir, we are here in search of our friend, a monk named Dorjee."

"Hu Xing told us that you may be able to help us find him. We really need your help," said Tony taking charge of the conversation.

"I welcome you both," said Norbu with folded hands and a smile.

"Please give me a day to find out about your friend. Meet me tomorrow afternoon and I hope to have some news by then," Norbu told them in a very polite manner.

"That's very kind of you, sir," said Krish.

"Thank you for your help, sir," said Tony in his trademark humble tone.

They also thanked Hu Xing for introducing them to Norbu and then left the council.

The next day as planned, they reached the council office in the afternoon. Norbu informed them that he had been able to trace Dorjee and that their friend was a monk in one of the monasteries in Lhasa. But three months ago, his father had died. So, he had gone back to his hometown Shigatse to live with his mother.

Hearing this news, Tony had mixed feelings. He was very happy to learn the whereabouts of his long-lost friend and would finally be able to meet him, at the same time he was saddened to hear of Dorjee's loss.

"Why don't you come over for lunch to my place today?" Norbu invited.

"You are very kind, but we don't want to bother you anymore. You have already done so much for us," said Krish.

"Nothing like that, in fact it will be a pleasure for me and my family to host you," he insisted.

They were unable to refuse such a polite invitation and agreed to join him for lunch.

At two p.m. sharp, Krish and Tony reached Norbu's home. He took them to the living room and introduced them to his family—his wife Nima, who was a teacher in a public school and his young and beautiful daughter Tashi, who was studying in college.

She was a very attractive girl with beautiful eyes, long flowing hair and a smile that could warm even the coldest of hearts.

Nima had prepared an elaborate Tibetan lunch and the duo thoroughly enjoyed the local cuisine.

Whilst having lunch they had an interesting conversation about Indian culture, pop music and Buddhism. They also cracked some jokes. Tony and Krish gradually became very friendly with the family.

Norbu asked Tashi to take the visitors to the local museum and show them some Buddhist artifacts. Both Krish and Tony readily agreed and decided to meet her the next morning at the city centre.

It was a perfect afternoon. They both left, thanking Norbu and his family for being such wonderful hosts. They invited them to make a trip to Mumbai so that they could show them some Indian hospitality.

Tony was very excited; it was one of the best days of his life.

It all seemed like a fairytale to him. He was in one of the most amazing places on earth, was soon going to meet Dorjee and he had also met this beautiful Tibetan girl.

Krish too was quite content with his day. He was very impressed with Norbu's benevolence and his family.

Having all the necessary information about Dorjee it was time to plan their subsequent moves.

The next morning, they went to the museum with Tashi. She showed them all the artifacts from different eras, patiently explaining their significance.

She also took them to a small Buddhist temple and introduced them to the priest.

It was a long day spent walking and sight-seeing. They had lunch at a Chinese restaurant, went for a long walk by the lake, followed by evening tea. Finally, it was time to drop Tashi back home.

Apparently, Tony and Tashi had started to enjoy each other's company and just didn't want the day to end. Like a true friend, Krish gave them some space whenever he could.

"Is it possible for you to join us on our trip to Shigatse?" Tony asked Tashi, mustering all of his courage.

"Only if you are comfortable," Krish added. He could read his friend's mind and wanted to ensure that Tashi didn't feel offended by Tony's request.

"Ahem, I would love to accompany you guys for the trip.

But you will need to seek my father's permission," said Tashi. She too seemed equally interested.

"Oh, yes. We will surely ask for his permission," said Tony trying to control his excitement. The mere fact that Tashi had shown interest in his proposal was encouragement enough for him.

When they dropped Tashi at her place, Tony decided to seek her father's permission.

"Sir, may we ask you for a favour?" asked Tony hesitatingly. He was quite scared as they had only known each other for a few days and didn't know how Norbu would react to their request.

"What is it? Please tell me," said Norbu in a kind tone.

"We were just thinking, since we don't speak Tibetan and are also new here, it might be a bit difficult for us to travel to a different city. Would it be possible for you to send Tashi with us to help find Dorjee?" interrupted Krish.

Deep inside his heart, Tony thanked Krish for this much-needed intervention as he didn't know how to ask Norbu for this.

"Well, not an issue. But on one condition—you will have to bring her back in three days," replied Norbu after deliberating the issue.

Both Tony and Krish couldn't believe their ears, things were happening as per plan.

"So, when are you people planning to leave?" Norbu asked.

"Tomorrow itself, sir!" replied Tony.

"If you have already decided for tomorrow then I would suggest you leave early in the morning," said Norbu. He asked Tashi to also pack her bags.

The lovebirds were on top of the world. They were getting a golden chance to spend time together.

Tony had never imagined that the search for his long-lost friend in the Himalayas would turn out to be so romantic.

Krish was happy for Tony and also because they now had a local accompanying them to this new place. Apparently, it was much smaller and less cosmopolitan than Lhasa.

The first bus to Shigatse left at six in the morning so they decided to meet at the bus stop a half hour before departure.

Though all the passengers were inside the bus at six, the bus started out after a delay of fifteen minutes, which wasn't really late by Tibetan standards.

"Are the buses in Lhasa normally late?" asked Tony.

"Late? Are you joking? A fifteen-minute delay is not late," replied Tashi pretending to be offended by his comment.

Krish wasn't surprised at this delay as he knew that in a lot of Asian countries even a half hour delay meant almost on time. But he chose to keep mum.

The seats were not too comfortable. Tony remembered the Mumbai-Goa ultra-luxury buses back home.

"Don't bother about the seats, you will forget the discomfort as we pass through the mountains," said Tashi. She seemed to have read his mind.

"I hear the view is breathtaking," said Krish.

"Yes, it is. The drive from Lhasa to Shigatse offers one of the most panoramic views," replied Tashi with a spark in her eyes. Her love and sense of pride for Tibet was quite visible in her body language.

Krish was enjoying the magnificent view of the Himalayas, appreciating the beauty of the snowcapped mountains and would get as excited as a child on spotting a yak by the road side.

Tony and Tashi spent their time talking about their lives, dreams, and also discussing their past.

"I am so in love with these mountains," said Tashi, sharing her passion for that place.

"Well, I live in a concrete jungle far from the mountains and have always been crazy for beaches. But now I love the Himalayas much more," winked Tony.

"True, and the best part is that a lot of it is still unexplored. That is why they call them the mysterious Himalayas," Tashi explained.

"Back home in Mumbai we are so engrossed with our busy lives. The simple, laid-back life here is so special. I feel so much at peace," said Tony as he looked lovingly at her.

Tashi gave him a warm smile and started looking out of the window.

The bus stopped midway for breakfast. The food joint was on top of the mountain giving everyone a bird's eye view of the valley.

After a thirty-minute halt, the driver honked as it was

time to leave. They reached Shigatse at lunchtime and were dropped off at the city centre. The temperature was much lower in this part of the world. The Sun was shining bright and the sky was clear but the wind made it a very chilly afternoon.

Norbu had arranged for their stay in the council guest house, where they were welcomed by the manager who showed them to their rooms.

Since it was a tiring journey, all of them decided to relax for the day and visit the monasteries the next morning. A quick lunch in the guest house was followed by the inevitable afternoon siesta.

The plan for the evening was to visit the nearby market.

"Folks, I will meet you at the guest house at eight p.m. for dinner," said Krish.

"Are you not joining us?" asked Tashi.

"Ah! Well, I want to spend some time by myself," said Krish as he wanted to give both Tony and Tashi some time together.

Tony chose to remain silent. He was aware that Krish was playing the part of a true friend.

"Shall we go to that café and have some tea?" asked Tashi.

"Sure! Nothing like a cup of green tea in the Himalayan valley with a beautiful lady," replied an excited Tony.

"Know what? In Mumbai we prefer coffee but ever since I landed in your beautiful country, I feel like having only tea."

"I am glad you are enjoying our way of life," said Tashi giving him a sweet smile.

"Shall we go to that garden after you finish your tea?" Tashi asked, pointing to the botanical garden which was about fifty meters from the council.

"Why not? Garden sounds great," replied Tony.

He wondered how she had managed to gulp such a hot cup of tea within a few seconds.

They enjoyed a lovely evening together and went back to the guest house. Seemingly, the friendship had blossomed into fondness for each other. Their lives had taken a different turn and they did not want their moments of bliss to end.

Krish reached the guest house quite early and spent his time garnering information about the monastery where Dorjee was living. He then proceeded to wait at the lobby for Tony and Tashi to join him for dinner.

They had some interesting conversations over dinner and Krish took this opportunity to tell Tashi about his culture.

It was time to hit the hay. They had to wake up early in the morning as this was the day Tony was finally going to meet his spiritual guru!

***

"Yogi, who is the one person that has influenced you the most?"

It was my turn to speak now.

"John, why don't you first tell me who your influencer was? And then I will share one of my most wonderful experiences," said my newly adopted guru with a radiant smile.

"Well, I have met so many celebrities, top athletes, businessmen. But I was most impressed by this self-made one-eyed tech billionaire who has a true rags-to-riches story."

"This man is truly a braveheart. Can't imagine how someone, despite being partly blind, raised in an orphanage, fought all the odds and ended up creating a technology behemoth."

"Trust me, it's not easy to run away from the shackles of poverty." I was hinting at my own struggles in life.

"That's true; the world is full of such dynamic personalities who had the courage to change their fortunes," Yogi reiterated.

"But I must tell you that the richest person I met was not a billionaire but a poor farmer in a small village. I met him while trekking in the Himalayas. The mere thought of that evening brings a smile to my face."

"Yes, I can see that. Tell me more," John requested.

"Well, I had gone for a short trek with my friends in the Himalayas. It was late spring, the best time to see the dense forest filled with rhododendron, pine, and deodar."

"We were having a surreal experience and the day was going just perfectly until I decided, midway, to take a shortcut to beat my friends. My strenuous training before the trek helped me reach the summit in less than two hours but, unfortunately, this was at another cliff. I had clearly lost my way."

"And guess what? It started raining. In the mountains there is nothing like 'rainy season.' It can rain any day of the year, especially if you trek above 9000 feet."

"Wow! How much would that be in meters?" I interrupted.

"Ahem! Near about 3000 meters. Since there was no shelter to save me from getting drenched, I decided to return via the same route."

"Rain and mist in the Himalayas are like fraternal twins—they may have different forms, but at any given time you have to deal with both of them."

"The rain had stopped, but due to the mist the visibility was so low that I again lost direction."

"Well, losing your way has its own benefits," chuckled Yogi. "And if you are lucky, you may end up discovering new peaks. After climbing down some 1000 meters, I reached a tiny village in the middle of nowhere."

"Cutting a long story short, this is where I was hosted by the great Shamlal, the kind-hearted villager who gave me shelter in his home as I was completely drenched and shivering because of the cold."

"It was getting dark. I was advised to stay in the village and leave for the base camp the next morning. Shamlal even assured me that he would send a message about my well-being to my friends who would be worried about my disappearance."

"Well, all the rain and fatigue couldn't drench my spirits and I wanted to enjoy every moment of that trip. I quickly changed my clothes and decided to engage in conversation with my kind host."

"What a night it was! We had such long and interesting conversations inside that smokey kitchen, sessions of ginger tea followed by dinner and then a hot cup of fresh cow's milk. Couldn't have asked for more."

"In a Himalayan village, the kitchen is like a quasi-living room and this is where important family matters are discussed."

"Believe me, that was the first time I felt so lucky to have lost my way," Yogi laughed.

"Shamlal had a family of five and all he owned in terms of wealth was two cows and a small piece of farmland. Just enough to feed his family."

"Intrigued by his happy state of mind, I asked him the reason behind his ever-smiling face. He gave me an answer in very simple words."

"Babu, nature provides all that we humans need. Everything else is unnecessary. Trust me, the best things in life are free."

"John, it's been decades but those simple words still resonate in my ears."

Without any T.V., computer, internet, etc. I wondered where he had gotten his wisdom from.

"If you ask me what his real wealth was, I think it was his sense of satisfaction, contentment, acceptance and his simple understanding of life."

"What an awesome experience, Yogi! I could actually visualize the entire scene. I am now adding a homestay in the Himalayas to my bucket list."

Chapter 7

It was a special morning. Everyone got up early, quickly finished their breakfast and left for the monastery. The plan was to reach there much before the morning prayers.

In about twenty minutes, they were at the monastery. They went directly to the reception and enquired about Dorjee.

The attendant advised them to reach the central hall at ten a.m. and said that they would find him attending morning prayers.

He warned them strictly not to approach Dorjee during the prayers.

Tony spotted his friend, dressed in the same yellow robes, sitting in the front row of the hall and in his excitement, he waved to him.

Seeing Tony at the visitors' end, Dorjee was shocked, but he chose to control his emotions.

Once the prayers were done, Dorjee rushed to Tony and gave him a warm hug. They both were filled with joy. For Tony it was no less than finding hidden treasure.

Dorjee had not expected to see Tony again after all these years.

"My friend, it's so nice to see you again," said Dorjee as he kissed Tony on his forehead.

"The feeling is mutual, my brother. I am so happy and proud to have found you at last," said Tony with a sense of achievement.

"I can't believe that I am here with you! You have no idea how many times I tried calling you on the phone number you gave me. I was never able to get through," Tony disclosed.

"My apologies, brother. It was only when I came back to Tibet that I realized the number I had given you was not working. Unfortunately, on my way back to Tibet, I lost my diary that held your phone number. I really wanted to be in touch with you but felt so helpless," said Dorjee with tears rolling down his cheeks.

Tony then introduced Krish and Tashi who were sitting in one corner and were smiling at the joyous faces of these long-lost friends.

"You must visit my home, it's close by. My mother will be very happy to meet you."

"We would love to meet her too. If we can come all the way to Tibet, your home in Shigatse is no distance at all," Krish replied.

"You know what? Your talks about a monk's life and the values you exhibited have left an indelible mark in my mind," said Tony. "And my keenness for Buddhism has only grown over the years."

"I am glad to hear that," said Dorjee with a spark of delight in his eyes.

"Mind you, a monk's life is not easy. There are no luxuries and comforts," said Dorjee. "We also have to follow strict celibacy."

"But I really wish to experience Buddhism," said Tony sounding a bit disappointed.

"You could do that without becoming a monk. I can introduce you to a Buddhist study school in Lhasa. You can learn more about our beliefs and begin to practice them too," said Dorjee.

"He is right, not all Buddhists are monks," Tashi intervened.

"I agree, joining the Buddhist school would be a good idea, Tony," said Krish as they all left for the hotel.

The evening was spent at Dorjee's home. His mother, a very affectionate and graceful lady, cooked special local delicacies for them, which they all enjoyed immensely.

Tony was surprised by their hospitality. After a sumptuous dinner it was time to leave. On reaching the guest house Krish held both of Tony's hands and said, "I am so happy that we succeeded in our mission."

"I thoroughly enjoyed our trip. As all good things must come to an end, it's time that I leave for home. I had promised my family I would join them in two weeks. They must be eagerly waiting for me."

"I can't thank you enough, my friend," said Tony with enormous gratitude as he gave him a tight hug. "This trip wouldn't have been a success without you. Thanks for being always there for me."

* * *

"How much time to the next station, Yogi? I am not used to sitting for so long. Need my small walks even when I am writing!"

"John, Bareilly is just an hour's distance from our last halt. We should be reaching there anytime soon. You can go down to the platform when the train halts, but don't take too long—the train stops there for only three minutes."

"Thank you, I will remember that."

The train left Bareilly at sharp 13:45 p.m. and I returned to the cabin after a brisk two-minute walk.

Our cabin attendant was back in action too. This time he brought our pre-booked lunch. Coincidently, both of us had requested pure vegetarian meals.

After twenty minutes of silence it was time for the conversation to resume.

Yogi was the one to start. He could gauge my interest.

"Know what, John? Bareilly is a small town but her name has a place in our history books."

"Queen Draupadi of the famous Hindu epic, the Mahabharata, was believed to have been born here."

"Yogi, I remember having read about this epic in my school days. Is it the same one where Lord Krishna talks about the importance of good deeds in our lives?"

"Ahem, another question!"

I raised my hand like a school kid.

"Do you believe that the Mahabharata is a true story?"

"Well, John, whether it was reality or the imagination of a very skilled writer, I leave it to the judgment of historians. I only have this to say: the way technology is progressing it is impossible to predict life in the future. Five thousand years from now the great events of today would have become legends."

"Travelling in a train or using mobile phones for communication may appear too primitive. Our lives may seem too simplistic to those generations. Some of them may even refuse to believe that we even existed."

"Now, let's get back to our story before that too becomes a legend," laughed Yogi in an attempt to bring me back to the present.

He had mastered the art of teleportation. I was being hurled back and forth from past to present and now even to the future.

Chapter 8

The flight to New Delhi was about to leave in an hour and Krish was sitting in the airport lobby waiting for the boarding announcement.

For him, Tibet seemed to have been the most surreal experience. He was leaving the Himalayan kingdom with many colourful memories. He was deeply touched by the politeness and generosity of the locals.

It was a four-hour flight and Krish wanted to reach Delhi as soon as possible. His wife and father were traveling all the way from Varanasi to receive him at the airport.

He was going to see his parents after a long time and couldn't wait to meet them. He had firmly decided to persuade them to move to Mumbai with him.

All his efforts in the past had failed—his father was from the old school of thought and wanted to spend the rest of his life only in his native place.

He zoned out thinking about his family and his deep thoughts were interrupted by the airlines announcing his name. He was deeply embarrassed. It was his final boarding call and he had to rush to catch his flight.

The small aircraft was full of Buddhist monks who, in all likelihood, were going on a pilgrimage to the famous Buddhist Circuit in India.

Lunch and drinks were served once the plane had reached a reasonable altitude, which in the Himalayas would be above 30,000 feet. A sip of wine with the view of the mighty Himalayan peaks was quite intoxicating.

In exactly four hours, the flight landed in New Delhi. It was a crisp winter evening and actually the best time to visit the northern part of the country.

"How was your journey, my son?" asked his father, giving him a warm hug.

"The journey was wonderful, dad. I am still kind of fresh," replied Krish as he stepped aside to hug his wife and son.

"You must be tired. Shall we stay here in Delhi for tonight? We can leave for Varanasi tomorrow morning," his father suggested.

"Not at all dad, it was just a four-hour journey and I am ready for another," replied Krish stretching his arms inside the car.

"India is fast changing, look at these high rises on the highway!" Krish exclaimed.

"Well! The development has just started here and honestly there's a long way to go," replied his not too convinced father.

The journey was long so they kept talking all night ensuring that no one would fall sleep. After ten hours on the road, they finally reached Varanasi. Krish's mother and daughter were eagerly waiting for them.

Visiting Varanasi after almost a year and seeing the whole family together was a very special feeling.

The next few hours were spent chatting over tea and snacks. The children were happy and excited about their gifts of toys and sweets.

"Life has changed in our small town too," said Krish's father with a deep sigh.

"I did notice a lot of improvement in the infrastructure," said Krish. "I see that development has reached this part of the country too."

"Huh, you call it development? People have forgotten moral values; respect and social bonding is missing. Everyone is running after money, and there is too much of Western influence here which is not healthy for our society," replied his father.

"Back in the day we were proud of Varanasi and its heritage as being one of the oldest cities in the world. But look at it now! It's slowly becoming a concrete jungle."

"You are right, dad. But the whole world is changing and we should also change with time or we will be left out," said Krish in a very diplomatic way.

Krish was also amazed to see how the entire landscape had changed in his native place— independent homes were replaced by apartment complexes and the sporadic growth of shopping malls in such a short time was unreal. Every time he would visit, the city would look different.

The one thing that never changed in 5000 years was the piety of the people at the holy river Ganges, popularly known in India as the Ganga.

Interestingly, Hindus all over the world still worshiped her as they did in the ancient times. Even today, a dip in the holy river was supposed to wash away sins and purify the soul. The scattering of the ashes of the dead in the Ganges, no matter how polluting, was believed to give salvation to the departed soul.

Krish was looking forward to a walk in the by-lanes of Varanasi and to visit the place where he had spent his childhood. Those were the days when he would go to the Ghats of the Ganges with his school friends and they would spend hours there, playing and dreaming about their futures.

The past few weeks had been extremely eventful for him. The trip to Goa followed by the airplane hijacking and then their trip to the Himalayan kingdom.

It all seemed like a dream, travelling from Sin City to the mysterious Himalayas and now back home in one of the oldest cities of the world.

The next few days were spent with his family. All the relatives met over numerous lunches and dinners, culminating in a family picnic over the weekend at the famous City Garden.

Krish now was beginning to feel stifled and felt strongly the urge for a break, but given the situation, that seemed like a distant dream.

One day while he was reading the newspaper, Mira came to the garden where he was seated and broke the news of the sudden demise of a distant relative of hers.

Voila, this was the moment he had been waiting for.

The funeral was in Allahabad, and finally he was going

to get a few days of peace and quiet. He was like a free bird wanting to fly in the open sky.

Mira tried to persuade Krish to accompany them for the funeral to which he gently refused, saying that there was no need for so many people to attend the funeral.

It would be extra trouble for the bereaved family.

The next day after the family left, he immediately took a rickshaw and headed towards the famous Ghats of Varanasi.

He purposely chose this mode of transport as he wanted to appreciate the changing landscape of his revered city.

On his last trip he could not visit the Ghats, as he had been suffering from typhoid and could barely leave his home. It was a huge disappointment to him, perhaps the first time that he had left the city without visiting his favourite place.

Krish started a conversation with the rickshaw puller called Bade Miyan, who turned out to be quite an expert on the social and political matters of this ancient city.

"How is life in Varanasi these days, Bade Miyan?" asked Krish trying to draw him out and learn his views.

"Don't ask, *Sahib*, it has gone from bad to worse,' replied Bade Miyan in a rather disappointing tone.

"Why do you say so? There is so much development happening here—there are new roads, flyovers, shopping malls, lesser power cuts and so many multinational companies opening shops which is also generating new jobs," Krish added.

"Sahib, what is the meaning of this development where the rich are growing richer and the poor are becoming poorer?"

"It is no longer the Banaras I came to thirty years ago. Today there are more rickshaw pullers and fewer tourists. Sometimes I think staying back in Lucknow would have been better for me."

"Where does your family live, Bade Miyan? Have you left them in your village?" Krish continued the conversation.

"Sahib, I am a married man and my family lives with me. I am the only earning member of a family of four. I have two teenage daughters; they both are studying in middle school. To tell you the truth, I am very happy with my daughters."

"Don't you want a son?"

"Huh! Who wants sons? You spend all your life pampering them. By the time they're teenagers, they would pick up the bad habits of smoking and drinking—not to forget the endless chasing after girls."

"When they are grown enough to share your burden and it is time for you to enjoy the fruits of retirement, some lady from outside will join the family and make us dance to her tunes."

"In fact, you would be lucky if you are able to spend your old age peacefully in your own house," said Bade Miyan.

"A daughter never changes towards her parents and loves them all through her life," he continued.

"Bade Miyan, it's nice that you are educating your

daughters but why are you so much against sons? You yourself are one. Aren't you?"'

"Yes Sahib. I am also a son. But our times were different. People had moral values and ethics," he replied.

"It's nice that you are sending your daughters to school," interrupted Krish, though he wasn't getting a chance to speak.

"Yes, Sahib, it is important to educate girls so they can be self-sufficient if required. After all, they have to get married one day and manage their families."

"I am working hard to ensure that my children have a better future—the rest is God's will. Life is really difficult these days," Bade Miyan complained as he wiped the sweat from his face.

Krish was surprised to hear such intelligent comments from a rickshaw puller and showed empathy towards him. This was the beauty of democracy; everyone had a view. The best part was that no one could stop you from expressing it.

On reaching the Ghats, Krish thanked Bade Miyan for that stimulating discussion and rewarded him with a generous tip.

"Sahib, if I get such generous tips even for a month, I wouldn't mind shifting back to Lucknow," said Bade Miyan thanking Krish with all humility.

***

"Lucknow reminds me of our penultimate stop," said Yogi, bringing the focus back to our journey.

"What a simple character that man was! Seemed more real than fictional. What say, Yogi?"

"Well, you must wait till the end of the story," Yogi replied with a straight face. He didn't want me to have the slightest possible hint about the genre of his story.

A brief ensuing silence was broken by a knock on the door. No prize for guessing! It was our ever-smiling attendant holding a tray in his hand.

"Tea time, sir! We also have toast and *samosas.* What would you like to have?"

"I would like to have the toast. How about you, Yogi?"

"John, have you ever tried Indian samosa?"

"Never dared to, am not a big fan of deep-fried food."

The very next moment he was looking at my beer belly.

"An evening tea is incomplete without a samosa and I insist that you try one."

I did not have the courage to refuse. I then gulped two of them in no time—they were too small by American standards.

'It's indeed delicious. Thanks for recommending this tasty snack."

"John, it may taste Indian but actually the samosa has its origin in the Middle East. By the way, Lucknow is famous for three things—the nawabs, the food, and the polite mannerisms of the locals. The most famous monument here, Bada Imambara, is a beautiful example of the far sightedness of the Nawabs."

"Would you like to know the story behind its construction?" asked Yogi.

"Yes, of course." Having spent almost eight hours with him, I knew Yogi would come up with another interesting insight. His attention to detail was baffling!

"Once, a severe famine hit Lucknow causing mass starvation. That is when the Nawab Asaf-ud-Daula stepped in and planned to construct a prayer hall. Not to impress the Almighty but to generate employment."

"Now here is the interesting part—while it was constructed by the commoners in the morning the elite were made to break a part of it in the night, thereby creating employment for both. Dating back 150 years, I wonder if this was the origin of Keynesian economics."

"That's very interesting and very heartening, Yogi. But how about the next part of your story? It's already 5:45 p.m. and we are only five hours away from Varanasi."

"Thank you, John, for bringing me back to the story. In fact, our next chapter is about Varanasi itself."

Chapter 9

The sun was setting. Krish, as always, was enthralled by the eternal peace of the Ghats.

This place was a visual delight. Such a colourful sight—pilgrims taking a dip in the Ganges to purify their souls, a group of tourists enjoying the crimson sunset, *sadhus* with matted locks smoking their way to Nirvana.

Having spent some time at the eastern corner of the Ghats, Krish started walking towards the main temple.

The magic of this place took him back to his school days when he would bunk classes to go to the Ghats and spend hours sitting by the banks of the Ganges.

His grandfather would never miss the evening prayers and usually had to bribe Krish with chocolates to accompany him to the temple.

While he was lost in all these thoughts, the temple bell rang; it was time for the evening *Arti*.

Evening prayers on the Ghats have always been an out-of-this-world experience—always swarming with devotees and visitors from all over the world. An air of sanctity cocooned all those who gathered there.

It never fails to be a truly overwhelming experience to see the rich, the poor, the ascetics, and the foreigners all gather at one place and surrender to the divine.

Melodious temple bells, the sweet scent of incense, burning *diyas* and sacred *shlokas* from the priests never fail to create an aura of spirituality.

The ceremony ended with the distribution of *Prasad*, which was offered to the deities first and then distributed to the devotees.

Krish just didn't feel like leaving that place and decided to spend some more time in the sacred ambience.

While he was enjoying the full moon view at the Ghats, his moments of eternal bliss were interrupted when a Caucasian looking sadhu came and sat beside him.

Dressed in an orange robe, ashes on his forehead and a beaming face, he radiated a blissful aura. They exchanged glances and smiled at each other.

"Hello! My name is Krish," he introduced himself out of sheer inquisitiveness.

"*Namaste*! I am Swami Mahesh."

"Oh, that's an interesting name. Where are you from Swamiji?" Krish asked with a trace of excitement in his voice.

"Son, I was born and raised in England but I took *sanyas* eight years ago. Have been living in Rishikesh ever since," replied the Swami. "How about you?"

"Well, I am very much an Indian; I belong to Varanasi but I am currently working in Mumbai. It is interesting to see so many Western tourists here, but how come you seem to have chosen the ascetic way of life?" It was Krish's next question to the-calm-as-a-cucumber Swami.

"Son, they are tourists and are interested in seeing the outer world. I am a sanyasi; my journey is to explore my inner self."

Swami Mahesh seemed to be very sure of what he wanted from life.

"That's interesting! But, can I ask how you thought of leaving your materialistic life in England and coming here, if I am not being too inquisitive?" Krish was trying to be polite with the Englishman.

"That's fine! Your questions are most welcome. My life is an open book. I have nothing to hide," replied the Swami with a peaceful smile.

"Actually, I am a doctor by profession and was married to a beautiful Indian girl. I lost my wife ten years ago; her death left a huge vacuum in my life that could never be filled."

"The next two years after her passing I tried to live a normal life but without much success. That is when I decided to renounce the world and move to Rishikesh to live a life of meditation."

"I joined a Gurukul in Rishikesh and stayed there for six years to learn Sanskrit and the Vedas. A year ago, I left for a pilgrimage and this is the last leg of my trip," continued the Swami.

"Wow, it is really interesting to know about your fascination for my country and our culture."

"Son, India is like a mighty flowing river, moving towards the sea of knowledge, accepting everyone on its way and taking everything in its stride."

"I believe the roots of this great country are very strong and that is the reason it survived centuries of foreign oppression and is still thriving."

"Look what happened to other civilizations—the Mayans, Incas, Egyptians, etc. They were equally ancient, advanced in writing, art, astronomy, and architecture."

"Egyptian architecture till today has no comparison, how they built those huge pyramids in the midst of a desert is still beyond our comprehension."

"Mayans had a great understanding of astronomy, even had their own calendar. But today they are no more than history in textbooks."

"I think the simplicity of the average Indian people, their respect for different faiths, and their acceptance of outsiders over the centuries is the reason why India has been in existence for thousands of years and will continue to prosper."

Krish was very impressed by the Swamiji's thoughts and found him to be even more Indian than himself.

However, it was time to go home. Krish thanked the Swamiji and took his permission to leave.

On the way back he thought about their discussion and it all appeared to be so true to him.

Surprisingly, it took a foreigner to make him realize the greatness of his own country and culture.

For the first time in his life, his western education and capitalist views seemed shallow.

For a moment he even thought of shifting to Varanasi for good.

***

"Tell me something about Rishikesh," I requested.

"Well, what can I say about the paradise of spirituality? It is one of the best places on earth for meditation."

"Sounds interesting. Would you like to share any special experiences?"

"John, there are many such episodes but I would like you to listen to this one. I am sure this will definitely surprise you."

"Once, I was travelling from Rishikesh to Varanasi. It was a last-minute booking so I could only manage to get a seat in a state-run bus that was leaving in the evening. The narrow seats, the uncomfortable and bumpy ride—nothing prevented me from falling asleep."

"A heavy dose of *parathas* and *sweet lassi* had done the trick; such was the magic of a heavy North Indian lunch—it could easily beat all the marijuana in the world."

"I dozed off the moment I boarded the bus and my lifelong dream of becoming a honcho came into play."

"The brief moment of my virtual success—celebrating a big corporate deal with a few Fortune 500 clients in the Bahamas—was ruthlessly broken by the sudden brakes applied by the bus driver."

"It was pitch dark outside and the single front light of the bus made it almost impossible for a human eye to spot the landslide. Our driver was drunk, and now he suddenly had the powers to see the invisible."

"By now everyone was out of the bus and thanked the

bus driver for applying the brakes just in time. A few seconds of delay and the bus would have fallen a hundred meters down into the valley, leaving all of us dead."

"I looked at the gorge again and thanked the almighty for saving our lives and then I started walking."

"The landslide had almost filled the entire road with rubble, leaving a foot of space which was only good enough for a motorbike to pass."

"This was so uncalled for, it was dark, and we were stuck in the middle of nowhere. The road was completely deserted and staying there waiting for some help wouldn't have been a wise decision."

"I thought of hitchhiking to the nearest town which, as per the driver, was some twenty kilometres away. I had only walked for ten minutes when I heard a bombarding sound coming from far and the very next minute there was a high beam piercing my eyes."

"Yes! It was a motorbike and I was praying that it didn't have a pillion rider on it. I started waving both my hands in the air and the next moment, the motorbike had stopped next to me. The high decibel noise of the Royal Enfield never sounded as melodious as it did in that moment."

"Interestingly, the rider was a sadhu, scantily dressed with matted locks and a long grey beard."

"Namaste, Babaji," I folded my hands and wished him, bowing at an angle of thirty degrees.

"Namaste, *beta*!" replied the Baba as he switched off the motorbike and lit his marijuana filled *chillum*.

"Tell me, why did you stop me?"

"Baba, my bus got stuck because of a landslide and I would be really thankful if you could offer me a lift to the nearby village."

"The Baba took a long drag and pointed towards the sky, 'Beta, be thankful to the Almighty who is running this show where we are all but actors. I can drop you near my home which is half a mile before the village. From there you will have to manage by yourself,' said the Baba as he put out his chillum and placed it in his bag."

"I controlled my laughter at the Shakespearean reference made by the Baba. Didn't want to offend him. He was my only ray of hope in that deserted place!"

"Without wasting a minute, I jumped onto the pillion seat. I couldn't have expected more interesting company than a marijuana-smoking Baba riding a motorbike out of nowhere."

"The Baba kick-started his bike and off we went."

"A few kilometres down and I thought of starting up a conversation."

"Baba, why do you smoke marijuana?"

I had to scream my lungs out, because the noise of the motorbike was no less than a rocket launch.

"Beta, we are the devotees of Shiva and have renounced the world. We smoke marijuana and meditate to attain Nirvana—there is no prohibition on smoking in our sect."

"What do you eat, Baba?"

"Beta, we do not eat like other sadhus, as our food is special," said the Baba as he looked back at me with a beaming smile.

"I was feeling thirsty and asked Baba if he had some water.

"He immediately stopped the motorbike, pulled out a black plastic covered bowl and gave me some water to drink."

"I gulped down the water in one go, thanked the Baba and carried on with my questions."

"Baba if you don't mind me asking, you said you have renounced the world, then why do you still have a motorbike? I have heard stories of sadhus traveling all the way to the Himalayas on foot but never heard of a motorbike riding hermit," I giggled.

"What is wrong with riding a motorbike? Eh? Are Babas not human?" he queried furiously.

"There are so many sadhus who proclaim to be *sanyasis* but live a five-star life, travel in jets and own a fleet of luxury cars. I am only using a borrowed motorbike to cover some distance."

"I soon realized that the Baba was feeling offended by such personal remarks and decided to keep quiet for the rest of my journey. I didn't want to jeopardize my ride."

"After twenty minutes of silence, the Baba stopped the motorbike and asked me to get down."

"I asked him, 'Baba why are you dropping me here? You said you would drop me near your home!'"

"Beta, this is my home. Remember I told you that the village is just ten minutes from here? You can easily walk till there," replied the Baba.

"But this is a cremation ground, no one lives here," I retorted in surprise and disbelief.

"The Baba replied, 'Beta, I am an *Aghori* sadhu. Haven't you heard about us? We live near cremation grounds and feed on half burnt bodies'."

"I was already scared to death and this sentence from the Baba sent shivers down my spine."

"I fainted when he told me that the round bowl from which I had the water was nothing but a human skull."

"The sunrise woke me the next morning and I found myself alone in the cremation ground, and the Baba was long gone. It was hard to believe that I had spent a whole night lying among burnt corpses."

"This episode was as scary as hell."

"Any other day I would have boasted of this incident to everyone, but that day I just wanted to reach the nearest village and catch the first bus to Varanasi."

"It was undoubtedly the most unforgettable day of my life, or shall we say my most unforgettable night."

"John, we have limited time and I have to finish the story. Shall we go back to where we left off?"

I slowly nodded. Once again, Yogi had managed to teleport me, this time to that pillion ride of the Aghori Baba.

Chapter 10

"How about a family trip to the theme park this weekend? Only if all of you are not too tired," Krish suggested.

"That's a great idea. It will be a nice change for everyone," replied Mira.

"Yippee! We are going to the theme park this Sunday!" Krish's super excited kids rushed to their grandparents' room and broke the news.

"I've heard the water park there has some really good rides," Krish informed them.

Krish would only talk about water rides as his fear for other rides came into play.

"Our Varanasi has really developed. A few years ago, one could not have imagined a theme park here and today we have a couple of them," Mira observed.

"That's fine. But what is the point of such growth when so many people can't afford even two meals a day?" Krish queried, taking a leaf out of the conversation he had had with Bade Miyan, the rickshaw puller.

"Krish, we have to understand that India is a much younger nation when it comes to development and competing in the international market. Life in general has improved over the years and poverty has gone down," replied Mira, sounding offended by his question.

She was such a patriot, no wonder she insisted on only living in India.

"And by the way, you don't have any right to complain," she alleged.

"Why? Am I not an Indian?" Krish was visibly surprised by her accusation.

"Well, it is because of nerds like you who get the best of education here and then leave the country to chase their international dreams," retorted Mira, shrugging her shoulders.

"What is wrong with dreaming big? And I am still in India, am I not?" Krish was visibly peeved.

"There's nothing wrong with it. But these dreams turn into our country's loss, the great Indian Brain Drain you see," Mira said in a conciliatory tone.

"C'mon Mira, you have to look at both sides of the coin. Those who work abroad bring a great deal of foreign exchange to our country and contribute towards the growth," Krish tried to reason with her.

"One can never win an argument with you," Mira laughed as she got up and went to the kitchen.

Krish was smiling as he knew they both were right with their points of view. More often than not, these intellectual discussions turned into arguments that would end up in a withdrawal from Mira's end.

On Sunday morning, as planned, the family left for the theme park. This time Krish couldn't avoid the roller coaster ride. Both the kids wanted to go on that particular ride with their dad. He was dead scared but kept his eyes open all through the ride as he didn't want to lose face in front of the kids.

Krish spent the next few weeks as a complete family man and then came the time for him to leave for Mumbai. The vacation was over and he had a lot of work to do.

Finally the day arrived, and he bid goodbye to his family and left for the airport. It was a midnight flight and Krish had reached the airport a couple of hours before departure.

That gave him plenty of time to shop, eat, and even take a little nap. But this time he decided to stay awake, trying to save himself the embarrassment that he had faced when his name was announced as a late passenger at the Lhasa airport.

Chapter 11

It was a beautiful, sunny day. The sky was as clear as the Caribbean Sea. Krish was happy to be back in Mumbai, though this time he hadn't missed it much. The trip to the Himalayas followed by his holiday in his hometown had been very special.

Krish took a cab straight to his office to meet his partner and get business updates. Barring his stay in Tibet, he had been regularly in touch with his partner and was keeping abreast of the company's affairs.

"Man, I am so jealous of you, you look so fresh and rejuvenated," said his business partner, welcoming Krish with a warm handshake.

"Oh yes, this was one of my best trips home. A real eye opener. You know, spending time with family is always so much fun, but I am equally excited to be back in office," said Krish as he sat on his chair, wondering if he really meant what he had just said.

"I can very well imagine that," said his partner. "Guess what? I have some news for you."

"What is it? Tell me quickly," Krish demanded impatiently.

"We have been approached by Alatel, the biggest telecom company in North America, to customize software for them," said his partner with a huge grin.

"Wow. Are you serious? Why didn't you tell me this before?" Krish complained. This is what he and his team had been gunning for. It was perhaps the biggest deal of his life.

"Well, I couldn't have. You were flying at that time. Got their email just last evening," winked his partner.

"Buddy, now it's your turn to take a break. A well-deserved one. I can't thank you enough for being such a sincere and understanding business partner. Especially for tolerating all my whims," said Krish with a sincere smile.

After an hour of discussion on both work and personal fronts, Krish called it a day.

His home bore a deserted look. Two months of abandonment can take a toll on the best of properties. Plus, having had to leave the family in Varanasi added to his depression. Krish quickly did some cleaning and in no mood to cook, he ordered his favourite wood-fired pizza.

Later that evening, he went to apprise Tony's father about their trip.

"Good to see you Krish. You had a real long vacation, eh?" said Tony's father with a lopsided smile.

"Yes Uncle, my longest vacation in years! How is Tony? Did you hear from him?" asked Krish unaware that a surprise awaited him.

"Guess he is still in Tibet. Last I heard from him was about a girl Tashi, whom he was madly in love with and planning to marry," said Tony's dad.

"What? Are you serious? Tony is marrying Tashi? That is so far the biggest news of the year!" exclaimed Krish.

"Do you know this girl?" Uncle was clearly not happy. His raised eyebrows spoke louder than his words.

"Indeed, Uncle. I was there when they met. In fact, we all travelled together. She is a real gem belonging to a very respectable family," said Krish remembering his trip.

"I am sure she really must be something. All these years I have been trying to convince your friend to get married, to no avail. Here he meets an Asian girl and decides to tie the knot in a matter of weeks," said uncle.

"So, when will the wedding bells be ringing?" asked Krish.

"I don't know. I haven't heard from him for more than a month and it is worrying me now. I wanted to check with you but had misplaced your phone number."

"Don't worry, uncle! Marriage is a huge event, and he must be figuring things out. You will hear from him soon. I'm sure," said Krish as he got up to leave.

"Have some coffee before you go."

"Thank you, uncle. But I have lot of pending work at home. Surely next time. Do let me know when you hear from Tony," said Krish as he left for his apartment.

Krish was the least surprised to hear about Tashi as he already knew Tony's feelings for her. Given their love for each other, marriage was obviously the next step.

It was time to find out about Asif.

The next day, after office hours, Krish went directly to Asif's home to find out how this friend was faring.

"Hello, Krish! How are you?" asked Asif's father, giving him a warm hug.

"I am perfectly fine, Uncle. How about you and Asif? Where is he these days? Looks like he has gotten very busy with his job."

"Oh yes! Ever since he returned from Goa, he has not only become a very sincere and hardworking man but also a very devout Muslim."

"He worked very hard at the auto store and became a top performing employee. His boss was quite happy with him so they sent him to Hyderabad for a week's training. But, we haven't heard from him for a month now and we are getting worried."

"Oh! Did you check with his company?"

"Yes, we did. But they denied having sent him for any training. In fact, he had not been reporting to work for almost a month before he left," interrupted Asif's mother as she started sobbing.

"We did not file any police complaint either as he had lied to us about his trip. We are dying to hear from him," said Asif's father, trying to console his wife.

Krish began to be worried now. His sixth sense was telling him that something was drastically wrong.

Krish said good bye to Asif's family and went home. His mind was a turbulent sea—thinking about his trip to Varanasi, Tony tying the knot with Tashi, and Asif's disappearance.

The mystery surrounding his two friends was too much for him to handle so he thought of calling Laila, the Tarot reader who had predicted a lot of things which had panned out correctly till now.

"Hi, this is Laila," said the voice from the other side.

"Hello Laila, how are you? Remember me? Krish? You were sitting next to my friend Tony on the flight to Goa a few months ago. You mentioned that we were special and even gave your contact number to him," said a disturbed Krish.

"Oh, yes! How can I forget you people? You are going to be the greatest testimony of my predictions. So, how are you? And where are your two friends? Are they already on the path to salvation?" Laila enquired.

"I am well and right now in Mumbai. What do you mean by the path to salvation? We haven't heard from both my friends in a while. Their families too are unaware of their whereabouts. This is very worrying!" Krish admitted.

"See, I told your friend that your lives were going to change the moment you left Goa!" Laila said, sounding quite proud of her prediction.

"Don't worry, you will soon get news from them, and yes, no matter what happens, keep up the good work. Remember, we all are born for a purpose and cannot leave this world without fulfilling it," she concluded.

"Thanks, Laila, I hope you are right," said Krish disconnecting the call.

Huh! Why can't this woman give me some straight answers? Krish mumbled to himself in sheer exasperation.

It was life as usual for the next few months.

Krish's family had arrived in Mumbai and he got busy on the big telecom deal, juggling work and family life.

Chapter 12

"How are your friends? Haven't seen them in a while," remarked Mira as she served evening tea. "They have been missing ever since we came back to Mumbai."

"Don't ask, Mira. There is no news of them," replied Krish taking a deep breath followed by an equally large sip of tea.

"What are you saying? Hope everything is alright?" Mira asked with alarmingly. She shushed the kids and sent them off to their room.

"Tony, I am sure, is still in Tibet with his lady love. But no one knows the whereabouts of Asif," Krish admitted with an air of defeat.

This serious discussion was interrupted by the doorbell. Mira got up to see if it was the electrician to fix the garden lights.

"Hey Krish, its Tony!" Mira came rushing to the living room, shouting at the top of her voice.

Krish jumped out of his couch and rushed to the door. This is what happens when you meet an absconding friend.

"Tony, my friend, where have you been? You had all of us worried," said Krish as he gave him a tight hug.

"I am so ecstatic to see you. Come on in. Let's have a cup of tea together."

"I am fine, Krish. Would you mind if we go for a walk?" requested Tony in a very mild tone. He looked tired and weak.

"Yes, sure. What happened to you, man? Is everything alright? You look so frail!" Krish questioned his friend while patting his shoulder.

"I am fine. I just need some fresh air. I have so much to tell you," Tony said as they stepped out of the apartment.

"I want to know it all. Look at you—you have grown so slim, I am sure you have been careless about your health." Krish protested.

Tony had shed quite a few pounds. The spark in his eyes had faded away.

"Where is Tashi? I bet she is your wife now," Krish was impatient and curious.

"I will tell you all," said Tony with tears in his eyes.

Krish held Tony's hand tightly and tried to calm him down. He knew something terrible had happened to his friend.

"Well, it was all quite surreal when you left Tibet," said Tony and a torrent of words spilled out of him. Thus, Tony began narrating his story:

The very next day, Tashi and I left for Lhasa by an afternoon bus. Dorjee had already spoken to the head of a Buddhist study school there and they readily agreed to take me on as a student. We reached Lhasa in the evening and went straight to Tashi's place.

Norbu was extremely relieved to see her back—he had been anxious about her absence. He was worried that the neighbours would start fabricating stories about her.

"Welcome back, I heard you found your friend, eh?" asked Norbu.

"Thank you, sir, yes, we did manage to find Dorjee," I replied and stepped forward to shake his hand.

"We also met his family. They are nice people," Tashi added.

Rounds of tea and snacks served by Norbu's wife added flavour to the evening and I was being advised to finish the tea before it got cold.

"So, what next?" asked Norbu.

"Actually, sir, I am planning to study Buddhism here in Lhasa. My friend spoke to the head of a study school here and they want to meet me tomorrow to complete the formalities," I told him controlling my excitement.

I wanted to behave like a mature individual in front of Norbu as I was going to have some serious talk with him.

"That is very nice," said Norbu's wife as she took the empty cups back to the kitchen.

"Why don't you go to your room and change?" said Norbu to his daughter, pointing towards the stairs.

Seeing Tashi leaving the room, I got a little nervous and started looking here and there as I didn't know where to start. Moreover, you, Krish, weren't there to handle the situation if it went out of hand.

"Sir, I wanted to tell you something," I finally managed to muster some courage.

'Tell me," said Norbu in his characteristically polite tone.

"Actually sir...ummm..."

"I am in love with your daughter and wish to marry her," I hurriedly blurted out. I was not sure how Norbu would react and I was looking for a place to hide my face.

"What are you saying?" said Norbu looking straight into my eyes.

We looked eye to eye for the longest time. I don't know where I got this sudden strength from. Perhaps by gauging it from his mild tone.

The very next moment he called Tashi back to the living room and asked her if she also harboured similar feelings for me.

She too confessed having fallen for me and that she was more than willing to marry me. To my utter surprise, Norbu immediately agreed to our marriage.

"My son, I am so happy to hear your plans to study Buddhism. My wife and I always found you to be a thorough gentleman. Any father would be happy to have you as his son-in-law. Welcome to the family," said Norbu as he got up and gave me a warm hug.

I could not believe my ears and felt as if I was dreaming. I even asked Tashi to pinch me to ensure it was all real. I had expected him to agree to our marriage but not so quickly and effortlessly.

Tashi too was surprised by her father's gesture. She had not expected her father to so readily allow her to marry someone whom they had met only a few days ago.

Our marriage was supposed to take place after a week and everyone was busy preparing for it. Tashi and I were in a different world. We were inseparable now and wanted to enjoy our period of courtship.

The sudden turn of events was baffling for me too. All these years my father was after my life to get married and I would always turn a deaf ear to his advice, so much so that he had stopped asking me altogether.

But now, here I was, all set to get married and that too to someone from the Orient.

Life was beautiful—our days started with a visit to the monastery followed by a walk in the shopping mall, and ended up at the lake side.

We would talk tirelessly all day long and Tashi would bombard me with her questions about my life in India, my profession, my past, my friends, and my previous relationships.

I would patiently reply to all her questions and would keep talking till she was completely satisfied.

We were head over heels in love with each other.

Evenings were all the more beautiful. Holding hands and walking by the lake, enjoying the sunset. Beautiful flowers surrounding the lake added to the loveliness, peace, and serenity which was omnipresent.

Those were indeed some of the best days of our lives. Then came the wedding day, which everyone had been eagerly waiting for.

It was a grand function. Norbu had organized a traditional wedding.

The bride's uncle formally started the wedding ceremony. Tashi and I knelt in front of her uncle and behind him was a picture of Lord Buddha, where the monks were chanting.

The ceremony was followed by the wedding feast which was thoroughly enjoyed by all the guests.

Tashi's father had made special arrangements for food and drinks, as this was the time to flaunt his prosperity.

He had hired the best cooks in town and also arranged for a dance troupe to perform the traditional Tibetan dance.

The kids were lighting fire crackers and the grown-ups were drunk and dancing to the local music, a new fad in Lhasa. Tashi's mother was busy collecting wedding presents. Gifting is customary in the Tibetan culture.

Norbu gifted me a five-acre plot of land on which I had started farming and Tashi had taken up a teacher's job.

We were having the time of our lives, simply not wanting it to end, ever!

Like any other couple, we were striving hard to make a good life. A life, although much harder when compared to Mumbai, but one filled with happiness and peace.

Everything was perfect until that one fateful day which took away everything from me and my life came to a standstill. Something shook my world in just a few, unbelievable seconds.

It was a Friday evening. As per my routine, I was ready to leave for the supermarket to buy our weekly groceries. It was an hour's distance away from our home and I always went there on my motorbike.

"Going to the supermarket, honey," I told Tashi as I was leaving. She was cooking supper.

"Ok. When will you be back?" she shouted from the kitchen.

"Don't you know, Tashi? Like always, I should be back latest in three hours," I replied as I kickstarted my motorbike.

Halfway there, the front tire of my motorbike developed a puncture. Luckily, a few meters ahead was a tire repair shop that saved me from having to drag my punctured motorbike right up to the supermarket.

"Sir, this is not a puncture. The whole tube has burst and you will have to replace it," said the mechanic.

"Ok. Then do change the tube. But please be quick," I told him.

"Sir, I am afraid I don't have a new tube for your bike. You can come tomorrow. I shall bring a new tube from the market and replace it," said the mechanic.

"You see, I am halfway from my home and can't drag the motorcycle back. Is it ok if I leave it at your workshop and pick it up tomorrow evening?" I wanted to save myself the trouble of dragging it all the way home. That's the best I could have done.

"That's fine, sir. But there isn't much space in my shop so please don't forget to collect it tomorrow."

I thanked the mechanic for his generosity and stepped out of the shop to head back home.

Walking all the way would have taken me hours so I decided to hitchhike, which wasn't a common way of traveling, but being an outsider, I thought I may come across some kind soul who would offer me a lift.

As luck would have it, I managed to get a lift from a kind old man, who agreed to drop me very close to my home. I was worried that Tashi would be disappointed to hear that I couldn't get her the weekly groceries.

It was getting dark so I hurried home. As I entered I couldn't believe my eyes—my wife was in the arms of another man!

I was dumbfounded to see her like that. My whole body was numb and my mind had stopped working.

All my dreams were shattered in that moment and my life fell apart. Tashi, whom I had loved like no other, had betrayed me.

"What is this? Who is this man, Tashi?" I bellowed.

"He is my lover," said Tashi shamelessly.

"If he is your lover, then who am I? You are supposed to be my wife," my voice was louder this time.

"Yes, I am married to you but he is the one I love," replied Tashi with no remorse.

"So, you lied to me about our love and all those dreams of a happy life together. Why you did this to me, Tashi?"

I could not believe that this was happening to me. In that one moment, my sweet and loving wife had turned into a cold, cruel stranger.

"Ha ha. Actually, love and marriage with you was just a part of my mission," said Tashi.

She had this wicked smile on her face.

"Mission? What mission are you talking about?"

"Well, I am a Chinese intelligence officer and it was my job to spy on you."

"Spy on me? Why would China need to spy on a man who has come to Tibet just to meet his friend and study Buddhism?"

I couldn't believe my ears. The woman I had trusted with my life had cheated on me. She turned out to be deceitful.

"You are an Indian and every outsider is considered a potential threat to Tibet's internal security. We had our eyes on you ever since you met those Buddhist monks in Mumbai."

"But they were just Buddhist monks whom I met only to find out about my friend."

"Well, for your information, two of those monks were on a secret mission. They were on our watch list as they were planning to create trouble in Tibet," said Tashi.

"We always knew that you are an undercover agent and you are here to spread unrest amongst the Buddhist community in Tibet."

"Your friend Krish was lucky to escape when he did, else he too would have been on our radar," she continued.

That's when I grasped the clear picture of the situation. I could connect all the incidents starting from my meeting with those monks in Mumbai followed by our trip to Tibet and meeting that English-speaking Chinese monk in the monastery in Tibet.

It was why that monk had introduced me to Norbu and why Norbu readily agreed to send his daughter to another city with strangers. The reason he didn't have any hesitation in marrying her to an Indian, and also why Tashi had asked me so many questions about my past and my profession.

"This is incredibly wrong! I am enraged to hear such comments about both you and myself! I can't believe that a woman like Tashi could have such fallacious tendencies," Krish interrupted.

"There was much more to it, Krish. But before we get into it, let's have a cup of coffee."

We went to a nearby coffee shop and had two shots of extra strong coffee.

"I am feeling much better after pouring my heart out to you, Krish."

Krish smiled gently and said, "I am curious to know what happened next."

After revealing her true identity, Tashi asked me to shut up or face the consequences. The very next moment, her lover pointed his pistol at me and took me into the bedroom.

He pushed me in and locked the door from outside. They said that they would be back in half an hour and that I shouldn't try to escape or they would be forced to kill me.

All hell broke loose when I saw them coming back with armed Chinese policemen. I could not believe my eyes; I had come to Tibet in search of my long-lost friend and to explore Buddhism, and here I was surrounded by ten armed policemen as if I was some fugitive.

I was appalled at the problems confronting me—it was too much for me to handle. I had read about Chinese police torture in books and now I was having nightmares visualizing myself in their torture chamber, hanging upside down like a rooster in front of the butcher.

I had heard about the presence of Chinese intelligence in Tibet but never found anything unusual in it, because no country in the world can survive without a secret service.

But it was hard to believe that an open-minded traveller like me could be perceived as a potential threat to a country's internal security.

They arrested me and took me to the police station. I was put behind bars, and this was my first ever prison experience and needless to say, it was a massively unpleasant one.

I was kept in a special cell which would normally be allotted to either horrendous criminals or terrorists.

What irony! I had never even killed a roach and now I was being treated as a dreaded terrorist.

This incident reminded me of what Laila had told us in Goa—it was the second time I found myself in such a situation. I asked myself: *after having survived a plane hijack, would I get lucky this time too?*

The situation was quite unnerving. I was in a different country and didn't know the law of the land. I could clearly see death looming large over my head and I had lost all hope.

In case of conviction, I was looking at a full life term or at worst, capital punishment.

I was cursing myself for having fallen in love with Tashi and trusting her. I had loved her to death but she had fooled me.

I couldn't believe her love and marriage to me were just a well-woven tool of espionage. This simple and innocent-looking girl had turned out to be the Chinese Mata Hari.

For the next three weeks I lived like a criminal behind bars, constantly hoping and praying for someone to come and rescue me.

For weeks, no one came to meet me and I had lost all contact with the outside world. I was also worried about my father as he had no idea about my whereabouts.

I was kept in solitary confinement and was not allowed to mix with the other prisoners, so the loneliness of that cell was harrowing.

The secret police would take me to the torture chamber and persecute me on a regular basis— tying me to a chair and beating me mercilessly with a baton.

They would jump on my legs and laugh at my pain. I was even tied to a pole and given electric shocks.

It was all extremely painful; I could not sleep after returning to my cell. My whole body would become a mass of pain. My soul, too, was in deep anguish.

I kept pleading with them, declaring my innocence, but they were unmoved. My painful screams and howling did not affect them one bit. After all, it was their daily job and they knew every convict claimed to be innocent.

The days seemed so long and the nights were never-ending. Then one day, the guards told me that someone had come to meet me. I couldn't believe my ears as no one knew about my suffering in this godforsaken place, and I had not been allowed to contact anybody outside.

God, I was so happy to see an Indian face. His name was David, he was an officer at the Indian embassy in Tibet.

I was delighted to see a fellow Indian who hugged me as if we were old friends.

"I am so relived to meet you. Please save me from this hell, I promise you I am completely innocent and they have wrongly framed me with the charges of espionage," I just didn't want to stop talking.

"Don't worry, sir; I am here to help you. Tell me everything about your trip here and also something about your past," said David, trying to comfort me.

I revealed the entire story to David. He assured me that it was his job to help out fellow nationals in Tibet and he would try his best to ensure my early release.

There was finally some respite for me and I felt that now my days inside the Tibetan prison were numbered. After three days, the guards announced that I was being released.

I was taken to the prison office, where David and his councillor were waiting for me along with Chinese policemen to sign the legal documents.

I held my head high and wanted to scream on top of my voice, "Go to hell, you Chinese rascals."

But somehow, I controlled my anger and quietly went out of the prison gates and thanked David for his help.

"I am so grateful to you for saving my life."

"That's my job, sir," said David, firmly shaking my hand.

"If you actually want to thank someone, you must thank this gentleman called Dorjee. He is the one who called up the Indian embassy and reported your disappearance," he revealed while starting up his car.

"He never came to meet us but was regularly following up with the embassy. I am sure he did not want to endanger his life," he further added.

"David, would you mind dropping me at the nearest travel agency? I need to book my air ticket for Mumbai."

"Sure. Why not?" he said, and we drove away.

Believe me, Krish, I was so glad to hear that it was Dorjee who actually saved my life. It was comforting enough to know that at least this time, I did not trust the wrong person.

I did not want to stay even a single minute longer in Tibet and booked the very next flight to Mumbai, which was the next day.

I packed my bags and called Dorjee to say goodbye and to offer my gratitude to him. I was indebted to him for having saved my life.

Dorjee told me that he did not do anything special and it was his duty to help me as a friend. He revealed how ashamed he was of Tashi's deeds. He hoped that this one bad experience would not give me hateful memories of the place.

Well, I took the flight to Mumbai and was finally back home. Till date, I have been in a state of shock and can't explain why all this has happened to me.

It took me a week to come to terms with reality. I had no idea that Tibet would be such a roller coaster ride for me. I was unknowingly playing a game of Russian roulette with my life.

Saying thus, Tony ended his story.

"Thank God! You have been saved yet again, my friend! I know it is not easy to forget what you have gone through, but let bygones be bygones," said Krish, patting Tony's back yet again.

"Now you must leave your past behind and look to the future. You should thank God for saving your life again and giving you another opportunity to start life anew."

"Yes Krish, I am trying hard to be in control," said Tony with a feeble smile on his face.

"What about you, Krish? How was your trip to Varanasi?" Tony enquired.

"Well, I had a great time back home with my family in Varanasi. Being back at the Ghats and the Ganges was spiritually very uplifting for me. I also met some interesting people and one man, Swami Mahesh, has influenced my thoughts. We had some very interesting conversations," answered Krish.

"That's good to know, Krish. So glad you are safe and well. What about Asif? Where is he? Did you meet him?" asked Tony.

"Well, I haven't met him ever since we left for Tibet. But I did go to his place a few months ago."

"Did you meet his family?" asked Tony with a worried look.

"I did meet his parents. They too didn't know his whereabouts."

"All they knew was that he had been sent for a week's training to Hyderabad by his company but that he hadn't returned even after a whole month. I reckon he isn't back yet, otherwise he would have definitely called me."

Amazed at Asif's sudden and lengthy disappearance, they both decided to go to his place that evening and find out if there was any news about him.

***

"Yogi, isn't it strange that the moment you feel in total control, life surprises you with its own plans?"

"John, a believer in karma does not think like that. This is surely debatable," replied the old man, raising his eyebrows.

"Reacting actively or passively to any given situation depends largely on our will and understanding of the situation. We always have a choice, and at every stage there are innumerable possibilities. Only in hindsight are you able to connect the dots and realize that everything happens for a reason."

"I respect your views, sir. But let me give you a situation here and you tell me in all fairness what comes to your mind first," I was in no mood to relent.

"If a spy betrays her loving husband, what would be your initial thoughts about her? Would you find her deplorable?"

"Is she a woman who doesn't understand the meaning of love? Or is it that she never loved him at all?"

"Ha ha, John, it seems that the tables have been turned and I am happy to see that you are in control of this conversation now. Honestly, I think Tashi was a strong-willed woman, maybe she loved him too, but her love for her country was above everything else."

"Sir, what are you trying to say here? Can you please elaborate?"

"It's very simple, John. Life is all about the choices we make."

"I think Tony chose the wrong woman and Tashi chose the right man. Now, let us get back to the final part of our story."

Chapter 13

"Wake up, my friend. It's time to rise and shine. We have to leave the Swat valley and enter Afghanistan today itself."

"Brother, how can you be so cruel? I was having such a wonderful dream," said Asif rubbing his eyes.

"You mean dreaming of a martyr's death?" asked Qais, expecting a reply in the affirmative from his newest recruit.

"Not really. I was camping in the middle of the Sahara on a cold winter night, surrounded by beautiful Persian women. A voluptuous belly dancer was entertaining me while I was savouring an exotic dinner."

"Don't you know that alcohol and women are forbidden to believers?" questioned a much-agitated Qais.

"True, that is reality. But I don't have any control over my dreams," replied Asif and burst out laughing.

"My brother, please don't let your mind wander. The time has come to fulfil your biggest dream."

Qais didn't want him to get distracted by any vices.

After all, Asif was his choice and he couldn't afford to lose face in front of the commander.

This was going to be the real test of their mettle, facing the NATO forces for the first time. In return, they were assured a good life for their families.

Asif's family in India had no idea that he was so far away at the Afghanistan border, arguably the most troubled and sensitive place on earth. A breeding ground for insurgent activities.

They had met a few months ago at an auto store in Mumbai, when Qais was buying a car for his father, a diplomat posted in India. He was quite impressed by Asif's persistence and conviction as a sales person, so he invited him for coffee after the deal was closed.

Asif was too excited by the sale; it was his first for the month and as a polite gesture, he readily agreed to his client's invitation.

He had this brotherly feeling after meeting an Arab, which was the turning point of Asif's life. In the beginning, he found him to be an extremist but gradually started appreciating his views.

Qais had succeeded in poisoning another innocent victim's ears with his Anti-West dogma and convinced him that the West was responsible for all the sufferings in the world.

Clever as a fox, he was a tall, good looking surgeon from Yemen who had studied medicine in Germany.

His charisma and fluency in English, Arabic, French, and Spanish made him one of the insurgents' best handlers. Asif was special to Qais and he treated him like his younger brother.

After their arrival in Lahore, they were quickly moved for a three-month guerrilla training which took place in the toughest mountain ranges of North West Pakistan.

Those were perhaps the most physically tiring weeks in Asif's life. They had been trained to mount an ambush, lay IEDs, and operate firearms, making them one of the most ferocious and tenacious of fighters.

Today, their moment of reckoning had come—they were going to sneak into Afghanistan. They had to be extremely careful to avoid the border guards.

"Congratulations brother, you are a trained recruit now," said Qais patting Asif's back with his strong hands. "Now you are ready to enter the actual war zone."

"May we all have success in our mission," shouted a rather excited Asif.

"Amen!" said Qais with a sigh of relief. The mere thought of martyrdom made him emotional.

Asif was very excited that he was finally going to enter Afghanistan, the land of the brave Pathans.

"This country has faced war like no other and has always been at the receiving end," said Asif as he washed his face with fresh, cold water pumped out of the land with a makeshift generator.

"Yes, my brother, the brave Afghans have been facing war for ages and are still standing tall," replied Qais.

"Even though Soviet occupation had ruined this beautiful country and then twenty years later, the bloody NATO forces attacked it, completely destroying it, neither could succeed in killing the never say die spirit of the brave Afghans."

"I wonder if the children born thirty years ago knew the meaning of peace. Their men are fighting ever since they were born," said Asif, quite disturbed by the destruction in Afghanistan.

"The NATO forces were blindly fighting the insurgents and had scant concern for the problems faced by civilians. The entire country was running on a parallel economy. Opium and arms were their only source of income."

"Brother, look at these people, there is no end to their suffering; they have no roads, schools, hospitals, no electricity, and no water. The West always complained about insurgency in Afghanistan but never tried to find the root cause nor a peaceful solution to it; instead they imposed a war on it," Qais spoke passionately.

"Tell me, brother, why is the West so insensitive to these poor people? Why do they kill innocent civilians?" asked a now incensed Asif.

"Well, why would they want to solve the problems they themselves have created?"

"Hurry up now. It is time for breakfast. Let's leave! We have a long day," said Qais cutting the conversation short.

All the recruits had breakfast in the Swat valley and then left on their journey to the Afghanistan border. Crossing the tough mountain ridges made their journey incredibly hard.

Although they were all well-equipped and had sufficient food to last them a week, their biggest challenge was to cross the border braving the continuous firing of NATO forces. After six hours of walking through the rough terrain, they finally reached the border.

All the way, Asif was praying for his success in crossing

the border as this was the first and the most crucial step on this trip.

He preferred dying fighting the enemy face to face, rather than trying to escape them.

Ambushed by the enemy guards on the fence, they were reduced to only half the number. Only ten of them managed to cross the border and half of them were severely wounded.

"Go Asif, run and save your life for our cause!" shouted Qais as he was lying in a pool of blood. He was hit by multiple bullets pumped into his chest by the guards.

"I can't leave you like this, my brother," said Asif with tears in his eyes.

"Don't be a fool. If you stay here, you will also die. Don't forget you are here for a purpose. Leave me and go," were the last words Qais spoke to Asif.

"Come fast, Asif," shouted his commander from the other side.

"Qais is dying. I cannot leave him like this," replied Asif.

"You fool! You will die too and put our lives also in jeopardy," shouted the commander as he came back and pulled Asif by his arm, dragging him towards the border fence.

Asif's eyes were stuck to the ground—he was watching his friend die and could do nothing.

Caught under heavy gunfire, they somehow managed to enter Afghanistan. Asif was happy to have cleared his first hurdle but was equally saddened by the loss of his dear friend. For the first time, he had faced enemy bullets and saw someone dying. He felt so helpless! He couldn't do anything to save Qais. They had only spent a few months together but had become like family.

It was a pity that they could not even arrange for his burial, a basic right of every human being.

The injured needed urgent medical care so the commander decided to halt at a nearby village.

Omar Kheil, a small hamlet with just ten houses, had a very deserted look. The commander knocked on the door of one of the houses which was opened by a middle-aged man. A true Pathan who was tall, well built, with a strong jaw line and deep blue eyes.

"What do you want?" asked the man in a stern voice.

"Who is the chief of this village?" asked the commander firmly, pointing a gun at him.

"Tell me. I am the chief and don't show me this toy, we have been playing with them since our childhood," said a visibly agitated chief.

"Sir, we have some injured men who need urgent medical care. Where can we find a doctor?" asked the commander in a conciliatory tone of voice as he had immediately realised his mistake.

The chief was unruffled by the AK-56, which was part of their daily life. He cautioned the commander to watch his tone while talking to Afghans.

However, on humanitarian grounds, he agreed to take the wounded to the village doctor.

The commander was amazed at the chief's audacity but didn't want to argue as the injured needed urgent attention and he didn't want to jeopardize the mission.

"Why does this village look so deserted?" asked the commander trying to break the ice.

The chief took a deep breath and said, "Omar Kheil used to be a very prosperous village, people from the neighbouring villages would come here to find work."

"Twenty years ago, there were more than a hundred families but today there are just ten left, because our village was ruined by this recent bombing in which most of the people died."

"A few lucky ones survived, because on that fateful night they had gone to a neighbouring village to attend a wedding. Now, we are trying to rebuild the village with the help of NATO forces."

"NATO forces? Why would they rebuild the villages that they themselves destroyed?' the commander queried in a satirical tone.

"Perhaps you are misinformed. The village was bombed by insurgents as they had false information about NATO forces hiding inside our houses."

"Without any warning, they indiscriminately bombarded the village leaving most of our people dead. Everyone lost one or more of their family members," said the chief with a huge sigh.

"We are trapped between the insurgents and the NATO forces and are forced to take up arms. The actual loss is of

Afghans—their families are dying and their children are becoming orphans because of this war."

"Actually, both the NATO forces and the insurgents are our enemies," said the chief. Asif was hearing the conversation patiently and was impressed with the village chief's persona.

This is what he had always visualised about Afghans. Their tough build and fearless character made them one of the best warriors in the world.

"Chief, what are those kids playing?" asked Asif as they were walking in the by lanes of Omar Kheil. He was trying to strike up a conversation with the Pathan.

"They are playing Buzkashi, our national sport," replied the chief with a smile.

"Is it an actual sport? Looks like horse riding to me," said Asif trying to ease the tension.

"Son, it is a simple game of the simple Afghan people. The players need to grab the goat while riding a horse. See those children sitting outside and watching the game? They did not choose to be spectators."

"They are the less fortunate ones—most of them lost their limbs stepping on land mines while grazing their goats in the fields. Still, they do not sport grim faces but are always smiling."

"The injured are getting treated, so we will stay in this village for a few days," said the commander to his recruits.

"Those of you who are in good health can go see the village, but be careful."

Asif couldn't have asked for more—the traveller in him was still alive. He wanted to explore the Afghan village and make friends with the locals.

That evening while he was sitting on a broken chair outside the makeshift playground, watching children play the game of Buzkashi, a young boy in his late twenties came and introduced himself to Asif.

"Hello, mister. My name is Noor."

"Hello, Noor. How are you?" replied Asif.

"I am fine, mister. You don't seem to be from this place."

"Yes, we arrived from Pakistan and a few of my friends are getting treated here," replied Asif.

"So, you are insurgents, eh?" asked the inquisitive Noor.

"People say that. But we would like to be known as warriors against injustice," Asif explained.

"Let me tell you this—we Afghans appreciate the fact that you recruits come from faraway places to fight for our rights. But it is important to understand that fighting this way will not yield any results," Noor reiterated.

This was the feeling of most people his age as they had never seen peace.

"It is really sad to see so many innocent civilians die. What do you do Noor?" said Asif trying to switch to a lighter topic.

"I don't do anything, mister. My father is a landlord, we have our own farms."

"You mean poppy farms?" said Asif with a wink.

"Yes, poppy farms. What else can we grow in this dry terrain?"

"Will you take me to your farm sometime? And please call me Asif."

"Ok, Mister. Oops! I mean Asif."

"Let's do it tomorrow." Noor was seemingly charmed by the visitor and wanted to know more about him.

The next day he took Asif to his farms. While the sun shone above them, they began to get tired and hungry so Noor invited Asif for lunch with his family.

"Oh! That will be very nice, nothing like spending some time with an Afghan family. Besides, I haven't had home-cooked food in a long time," said Asif, as nostalgia for food cooked by his mother engulfed him.

Noor introduced his new friend to his warm and welcoming family. Asif relished the Afghan delicacies cooked by Noor's mother but the best he liked was the dessert made by Henna. Henna was Noor's beautiful cousin.

She had been living with his family ever since she lost her parents to the war. She was indeed a real Afghan beauty, bestowed with glowing skin, long black hair, and emerald eyes.

Asif fell in love with her the moment he saw her. He was looking forward to spending some time with her, even if he had to make excuses to go to Noor's place just to get a glance of her.

Days passed by and Henna too began having feelings for Asif. One day they both confided in Noor.

They would often take his help to meet each other. Unperturbed by the ongoing war, they loved spending a whole day on the mountain, running and singing in the fields. They would come back only after the sunset.

No-one doubted their growing closeness as Noor would always accompany them.

"I miss my parents so much. I was too young when I lost them. The war took my childhood away from me. No one can understand the pain of being an orphan," said Henna, tears rolling down her cheeks.

"Control yourself, my love. No one can undo the past. May their souls rest in peace," said Asif as he wiped away her tears.

"This is why I hate war. I want to run away from this place," said Henna.

"Henna, to tell you the truth, I came here to fight against the NATO forces, but after seeing so much bloodshed of innocent people I am confused. Having witnessed the suffering of the Afghani people, I too am unsure about the results of our mission."

"I do not doubt the intentions of the martyrs, but it does not seem to be yielding any positive results for you people."

"You are right, Asif. We need good schools, hospitals, roads, etc. and not bloodshed. It is so disheartening to see young children losing their limbs and precious lives to landmines and bomb blasts."

"A good hospital would have ensured proper treatment for them and so many innocent lives could have been saved. You should also leave this war—it will only cause more destruction and loss of human life," urged Henna.

Asif was confused and at a loss for words. He had fallen in love with the place and its people. He found himself stuck between his loyalty to the mission and his love for Henna.

One day, Henna told him that they could run away and get married, and that her cousin would make the necessary arrangements for their escape.

"Run away and marry? Are you mad, Henna? The commander will kill us all even if he gets a hint of this plan," exclaimed a shocked Asif.

He held her hands firmly in his and told her, "Look Henna, I cannot risk your life."

"But I do not want a life without you Asif," replied Henna with tears in her eyes.

"I have a friend in the neighbouring village whose husband is a priest, he can get us married and then we can live a peaceful life," she pleaded.

Asif was in love with Henna and wanted to marry her. He had come to this war zone to become a martyr. But after meeting her, he too wanted to live a normal life.

While they were sitting together by the fields imagining their future, Noor came running towards them.

"What is it, brother? You look very excited," Henna asked.

"Sister, you will be equally thrilled on hearing the great news."

"Catch your breath first and then talk," Asif advised.

"Well, a Russian circus troupe arrived in our village this morning and they are going to perform here. I have already bought three tickets for tonight's show."

Henna was already jumping with joy.

"It is just a circus, what is so exciting about it?" asked a perplexed Asif. It was strange to see them so ecstatic about a circus.

"You will not understand, Asif. There are so many ways for recreation in your country. But here in Afghanistan, we have only Buzkashi and an old radio station in the name of entertainment."

"A circus, especially with Russian performers is definitely a great deal of fun for us." Henna had managed to explain a difficult situation in a very subtle manner.

However the Russian circus was a real mess. The tents were ripped and the ropes were frayed. The trapeze artists balanced on rickety boards and seemed nervous and the tightrope walkers swayed only five feet above the ground.

The audiences were watching the performance with their eyes glued to the stage. Everyone laughed at the clowns' slapstick antics and clapped when the announcer told them to.

A slightly older boy lit a cigarette with his feet, a man dressed up as a frog was hopping around and another one was riding a tall unicycle. After an hour-long performance, everyone came out laughing and beaming with joy.

"This is truly an international circus," said Noor.

"Well, it may have international performers but they are not really of an international standard."

"Nevertheless, it met the purpose, which was entertainment." Asif had noticed the frown on Henna's face and was quick to change his sentiments.

Henna just threw him a grateful smile and kept walking.

"Hey! Tomorrow is Eid, and you are invited to my place for lunch with my family," said Noor breaking the silence.

"Wow! That will be really nice," said Henna.

"Last Eid I was with my family. We had invited all my friends to my place for a feast." Asif was getting nostalgic about his family and his life in Mumbai again.

"Tomorrow, there will be no gun fire and no bombing as both the NATO forces and insurgents have declared a ceasefire for the day," Noor informed them.

"At least there will be one day when no one will die," replied Asif who had developed an intense bonding with the Afghans.

Eid was celebrated with much fervour in the village. Noor's father, being a rich landlord, had made lavish arrangements and all close friends and relatives were invited.

The men were dressed in newly stitched Afghani suits and the women wore colourful dresses and makeup imported from Pakistan, though they don't ever get a chance to show their face to men other than the ones in their families.

Everyone was all praise for the delicious and elaborate lunch—the specialty being the meat and rice cooked in an earthen pot, together with some exclusive eastern spices.

Asif's new friends had kept him so occupied that he didn't realize that two weeks had passed since he entered the village.

Now came the day of reckoning.

"We are leaving tonight after dinner. Our target is the NATO base which is ten kilometres from here," the commander told his recruits at the breakfast table.

The plan was to climb the mountain near the enemy headquarters and attack them in the wee hours of the morning to cause maximum damage. Although they were few in number, their spirits were very high.

Asif had different plans. He no longer wanted to fight this endless war and had secretly decided to run away and marry Henna.

Noor was requested to make all the necessary arrangements and to bring Henna to his farm in the afternoon.

Asif's heart was beating very fast as he went to the commander. "Sir, may I go meet my friend Noor for the last time? I shall be back by four p.m."

"Young man I see you have made a lot of friends here. You may go, but make sure you are back on time."

Asif thanked him and quickly left for Noor's place.

"Why are you late? I have been waiting for almost an hour," said a worried Asif.

"I am sorry, my love. I was waiting for everyone to go for their afternoon nap so that nobody sees us leaving this place," said Henna.

"Oh! That's okay. Let's not waste any more time. Every second is precious," Asif urged.

"You are right, Asif. Both of you must leave quickly and try to reach the neighbouring village as soon as possible. The commander and his team will start hunting for you the moment they know you have eloped," said Noor.

"I am scared," said Henna as she held Asif's hand tightly.

"Don't worry, sister. God is with you," said Noor, as he kissed Henna on her forehead.

"Noor, I need to ask you for another favour," said Asif.

"Tell me brother, what can I do for you?" asked Noor.

"If I die, will you post this to my family in Mumbai?" said Asif giving him a letter that he always carried in his pocket.

"I know nothing will happen to you, my brother. But I will still keep it for your satisfaction," said Noor as he took the letter from Asif and put it in his pocket.

"Take care, my friend. If God wishes, we shall meet again soon," said Asif as he hugged Noor.

Henna and Asif hurriedly left.

"Our life is going to change once we reach the village," said Henna holding Asif's hand as they were walking past the farms.

"Let us hope and pray we are able to reach the village safely," replied Asif. He didn't want to be overconfident.

"We will get married and have our own family. You will go to the farms and come back tired in the evening. I shall cook food for you and take care of the family. Life will be so beautiful with you, Asif." Henna was looking forward to the future.

"Yes, Henna. But for that we have to speed up and try to reach the village as soon as possible," said Asif, urging her to walk faster. "The commander will send the recruits in search of me the moment he realises that I have escaped."

"But we still have time, Asif. It is only three p.m. and you had promised to return by four," said Henna.

"Don't forget we have to save ourselves from the NATO army as well," said Asif.

It was a tough hilly terrain but the urge to survive and start a new life together gave them the impetus and the much-needed strength to continue their journey.

"We have been walking for hours now. Can we rest for a while?" asked Henna. She was tired and hungry.

"Let us go to that cave. We can sit there for some time and also eat," said Asif pointing to a cave which was about hundred meters away. He knew it wasn't safe to break journey midway but he couldn't stand to see Henna in pain.

"I think you are right. That place looks much safer for a stopover," said Henna.

"Shhhh...Can you hear that noise?" asked Henna.

"Yes. It sounds like an Army drill," replied Asif as he

got up and tried to peep out from the cave. "Oh my god..." he whispered.

"What's wrong?" Henna whispered back as she pulled him further into the cave.

"It's the NATO army, and they are coming this way," said Asif.

"What can we do now? Shall we run?" asked a worried Henna.

"If we go out of the cave, they will see us. We can only stay inside and pray and hope that they don't come into this cave," said Asif as he asked Henna to sit quietly in a corner.

"What if they spot us? What will happen to our dreams of a good life together?" said Henna as she started crying.

"Don't worry, my love. God is with us. We have reached this far safely and He alone will take us to our destination," said Asif as he hugged her tight.

It was a small troop of ten soldiers and two officers. They had received some intelligence about the insurgents in Omar Kheil and were planning to encounter them.

Asif and Henna were stuck inside the cave hiding in a corner. The best they could do was to pray for their lives.

As the soldiers crossed the cave, one of the officers asked them to halt as he spotted the fresh footprints in the sand leading into the cave. He was a young Major and was in charge of the troop. He ordered the soldiers to go inside the cave and check if there were insurgents hiding there.

Two soldiers carefully entered the cave and spotted Asif and Henna.

Guns were pointed at them. “Sir, there are two civilians inside,” shouted one of the soldiers from inside the cave.

“Bring them out,” said the Major.

Both Asif and Henna were handcuffed and brought out of the cave.

“Who are you?” the Major questioned Asif.

“Sir, we are civilians and we are going back to our village,” replied Asif.

“Why were you hiding inside the cave?” he asked, looking at them with suspicion.

“Sir, my wife was not feeling well so we stopped to rest for a bit here. Since there are insurgents everywhere, we took refuge inside the cave.”

“Where are you coming from?” was the Major’s next question.

“We had gone to attend a relative’s wedding in Omar Kheil village,” replied Asif.

“Omar Kheil?”

“Yes, sir.”

“We heard there are insurgents hiding in that village,” said the Major. “Did you see them?”

“Sir, I too heard about them but I think they have already left for Kabul,” replied Asif trying to save his friends. Although he was no longer a part of their mission, he was still concerned about their lives.

“Tell me, how many insurgents were there in Omar Kheil?” asked the Major in a stern voice.

"I think they were fifty in number and were heavily armed," replied Asif in an attempt to demoralize the charging NATO troop.

"Sir, he is lying."

"Our information says they are just ten of them. Are you also one of them?" screamed a sergeant, hitting Asif with the butt of his gun.

"No, sir, we are simple villagers," Asif replied. "We have nothing to do with the insurgents. We had gone to Omar Kheil only to attend a wedding and heard about their presence in the village."

"Please let us go," pleaded Henna.

"Sir, I think they also belong to the group of insurgents," said another sergeant.

"You are right," said the Major pointing his gun at Asif. "I would have let you go but your Indian accent got you into trouble."

He ordered two of his soldiers to take them to the nearest NATO army base.

The rest of the troops started marching towards Omar Kheil.

***

"Now that you have finished could you please tell me if it is a true story or a work of fiction?" I was quick enough to break the pause, not wanting to waste the last few minutes of our journey.

"John, what if I tell you that it's real fiction?"

"Real fiction? Sounds like an oxymoron," I replied with raised eyebrows.

Yogi started laughing. I didn't know if it was my facial expression or my choice of words.

"Well, the story can be real even if the characters are fictional," he replied with a most pleasing smile.

"This is the story of every human being ever born on earth. Krish, Tony, and Asif are nothing but the three most essential components of our lives—worldly desire, urge to seek the truth, and love of our beliefs. We all experience them at different times in our lives and the path we choose to attain them determines our destiny."

"I am sorry, Yogi. I am totally confused here. Can you please elucidate?"

"Ok. Let me put it this way. Like Krish, most of us yearn for success all our lives but later realize that a materialistic life can give comfort but real happiness lies in our spirituality."

"Tony was a seeker and travelled to a new place in search of truth, ultimately to come back and find his nirvana where he belongs. Every human being goes through this phase of detachment from their real lives, trying to find solace in the unknown. Only when we look in hindsight are we able to connect the dots and appreciate the reason for our existence."

"Asif was madly in love with his belief. He did realize that reality was far from what was preached, but it was too late for him. His obsession got him into trouble. Anything that we have more than our need becomes a toxin for our mind."

"Life is like an old-fashioned cocktail and you are the bartender. A perfect drink will need a balanced mix of all the ingredients."

"Thank you, Yogi! This has been such an enlightening journey for me. It would be an honour for me to write and publish this book for you. Here is my contact number. I shall wait to hear from you."

"John, you already know the story so you won't need me now."

I never heard from the mystic again. But his last words of wisdom are still fresh in my mind. "Knowledge is like a baton, and we have to keep passing it on to win the race."

Acknowledgement

Getting your first book published is like a dream come true and it only became possible with the contribution of so many amazing people in my life.

I would like to start by thanking my parents for their blessings, love, and support.

To my wife, Pooja, for her enduring trust in my story and perseverance in reading the early drafts. She was as important to this book getting done as I was. Thank you, dear.

To my son, Yuvan and daughter Anayra, for always keeping me cheerful, while I was struggling to get the editing right!

To my parent-in-laws, for their blessings and continued guidance.

To my sister, Sheetal, my brother-in-law, Amit, and my niece, Naaisha for their love and encouragement throughout.

To my friends, who have always stood by me and kept me motivated throughout the journey.

To everyone in the Nuvoice team—I can't thank enough my editors Vedika Paliwal and Navya Singh, Archita Purohit from the marketing team and Tarun Singh Negi for the great cover design.

And to all the readers, you are the reason I write.

About the Author

Vikram is a banker, author, and an angel investor with a background in Finance and Entrepreneurship. He co-founded Renaissance Investment Advisors after working in leadership roles at L&T Finance and HDFC Bank. He also shares his expertise as a guest faculty at top business schools in India.

Vikram has written two bestselling novels. His debut, Mystery of the Urban Monks, became an Amazon #1 bestseller and was featured by Outlook India as one of the "Top 10 Books That Will Change Your Outlook on Life." His second book, The Royal Abduction, also topped Amazon's Hot New Releases list. He regularly writes for business magazines, covering topics like startups, AI, and leadership.

Originally from Jammu and now based in Delhi, Vikram is passionate about travel and adventure, having trekked in the Himalayas. He also advises the IINREM Foundation, an NGO focused on community development, and holds advanced degrees in business from ESC Grenoble, France, and Pune University.